SHATTERED WINGS:

DIARY OF A CHILD BRIDE

*"Born with shattered wings, I never learned to fly.
I never knew how it felt to be loved as my life was
taken away from me before it even started, as I
became a child bride."*

Ann Marie Ruby

Disclaimer:

This book ("*Shattered Wings: Diary Of A Child Bride*") in no way
represents or endorses any religious, philosophical, political, or
scientific view. It has been written in good faith for people of all
cultures and beliefs. This book has been written in American English.
There may be minor variations in the spelling of names and dates due
to translations from Dutch, Bengali, and Hindi, or minor discrepancies
in historical records.

This is a work of fiction. Names, characters, places, and incidents are
the product of the author's imagination or are used fictitiously. Any
resemblance to actual persons, living or dead, is purely coincidental.
While the cities, towns, and villages are real, references to historical
events, real people, or real locations are used fictitiously.

Published in the United States of America, 2023.

ISBN-13: 979-8-9875085-6-5

DEDICATION

"Tomorrow, let dawn break open as you find new hope glimmering through the first rays of the morning sun. Let the doors of knowledge open as you enter the school room with books in your hands, not teardrops you have collected through the torturous nights."

Families rejoice over the birth of a child with laughter and joy. Children are the most innocent beings on Earth, yet so many more girls than boys are affected by child and forced marriage, also known as CFM. This is a humanitarian crisis and a human rights violation. How could this act be humane as a child is being forced to cut their childhood short?

Child marriage is not a religious issue as in countries like India, Bangladesh, Pakistan, Nepal, Niger, Burkina Faso, and Ethiopia, girls from Muslim, Hindu, and Christian families are married off as they are otherwise believed to be a burden. Globally, this action has inexplicably affected young girls and women. In South Asia, one in four women are married off before the age of eighteen. According to the United Nations Children's Fund, or UNICEF, Bangladesh alone has thirty-eight million child brides. In India 1.5 million girls under the age of eighteen are married off each year.

The state of New York passed a bill called Naila's Law after former Governor Andrew Cuomo signed it into legislation. Naila's Law raises the age of marriage to eighteen. This was the effect of a Pakistani-born woman named Naila Amin who is now an adult yet became a child bride at the age of thirteen. Yes, think about it. She was married at thirteen.

A very tragic reality awaits a lot of girls who come from around the globe to the United States as child brides whose grooms are much older than they are. These child brides fear their own family members who had them married off for financial, religious, social, or other entrenched reasons. These girls are prisoners in their own countries and even in the land of the free where they come as prisoners.

The girls who are married and pretend to be living happily are also being forced to give up their education, their freedom to make mistakes and learn, and their right to be an individual as they are always standing in another person's shadows, hidden from all. It's because they are told this is the way it is done so they don't make mistakes.

Yet they never share their stories as they would then become victims under the hands of their protectors. They are brought up to believe they are a burden and by becoming a child bride, they would be free from being the family's burden. Little do these girls know, they would now become the burden of their much older husbands to whom they are married off. Forever, these women are brought up to do as they are told, not as they wish.

Here in the United States, the minimum marriage age is sixteen in most of the states, yet in Hawaii and Kansas, the age is fifteen. Five states have no age limit, so a child could be married off at the age of zero. Ten states have banned child marriage all together.

This world seems to ignore its own girls, sisters, and mothers from whom you the children are all born. Discrimination laws have included so much now that we find ourselves a lot of helping hands in the legal systems around the globe. What happens when no one is breaking the laws of the lands? Yet you are taking away the basic human rights and self-dignity of children around the world.

They are signed off through the legal systems and sent away by the hands of their parents to live a life of misery and mortification. The reason is they were all born as girls, not as boys. So because of their gender, they are all being sent away or being sold to the highest bidders. I ask this world, why is it you are all still silent and why does your inner heart never think about these children from around the globe?

I do hope this paranormal fictional book awakens your inner heart even if the true stories from around the globe have not. Sometimes it takes a fictional character to come and knock on your doors for you to realize you have just missed one of the biggest humanitarian crises of this world.

I welcome you all to hold on to the hands of my fictional character Ahana. Walk with her as she holds on to the hands of the Kasteel Vrederic family members and finds the courage to share her life story and rewrites her own destiny. Yes, in my created world, Kasteel Vrederic, we always find a way out as the paranormal world is where dreams do come true even though in this world, the characters must still fight the hard life of reality.

I dedicate this book I call *Shattered Wings: The Diary Of A Child Bride* to all the victims of this humanitarian crisis of the young girls and the young women who had become a child bride far too early without their consent.

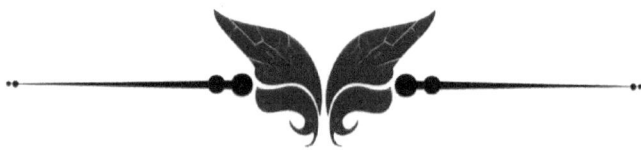

TABLE OF CONTENTS

BEHIND THE STORY:

The Paranormal Family Of Kasteel Vrederic

"Where a love story begins and where and when the story finishes is only known to the future readers of the story, not the participants who write the story with their lives."

Shattered Wings: Diary Of A Child Bride takes place in the same world as the Kasteel Vrederic. Here is a short preview of where this diary was born. In every world, some stories go missing as they get lost in the unknown places of history. The story of Ahana Roy, a child bride, had begun in the sixteenth-century Kasteel Vrederic, in Naarden, the Netherlands which at the time was overwhelmed by the Dutch Eighty Years' War. Kasteel Vrederic, home of the famous Dutch diarist Jacobus van Vrederic, on top of being ravaged by war, also faced the unjust sixteenth and seventeenth-century witch hunts.

At the time, a lot of women were unjustly being accused of being a witch. Yet through all the travesties and sorrows of life, this castle had given birth to many love stories which continued to take birth from the sixteenth century through the twenty-first century. This family is famously known as a paranormal family. Here within this world, reincarnation is a blessing. Dreams are guidance from the beyond. Time travel too is a top-secret mission as it's hidden within the walls of the castle. Immortality is not a dream anymore as it has been given to this family.

The first story began with a famous diarist, a devoted son of a wealthy man who found his beloved yet lost so much more. He still taught us there is more to life and not to give

3

up on hope as it makes life worth living. He was a beloved member of the society. As known in the second diary, with the help of Kasteel Vrederic's famous twin flames, the spirits of Kasteel Vrederic, and from his own will, he saved hundreds of innocent women from being hung at the gallows and from being burned at the stakes.

During the Dutch Eighty Years' War, the Kasteel Vrederic family helped whoever needed help, regardless of which group they belonged to. The Spaniards and the Dutch revolutionary soldiers loved Jacobus van Vrederic and took shelter in his home whenever they needed to. Yet in every love story, there are tears, loss of life, birth of life, joy, villains, and heroes.

In the seventeenth century, Ahana the female lead of this diary, was rescued from the gallows as she was accused of being a witch by someone she had healed from a grave illness. Jacobus rescued her with his wife Margriete and many other women who were all innocent yet accused by people to be a witch. At times, the reason was as simple as jealousy. After rescuing Ahana, Jacobus introduced her to Frederic van der Bijl, a Dutch Naval Captain, during the Dutch Eighty Years' War. Afterward, Jacobus had kept them in his home where Ahana trained to be a healer. With the help of the famous Kasteel Vrederic family, Ahana took this love as a profession and tried her best to heal all she could.

Yet the Dutch Eighty Years' War took as victim the famous diarist who was shot in the back and died. His beloved wife Margriete too had died from multiple bullet wounds as she fought her husband's attackers. Her death came faster as she was grief-stricken by being separated from her twin flame. They were laid to sleep together. The war had also taken their only daughter and son-in-law, the famous twin flames and the spirits of Kasteel Vrederic. The only surviving heiress of Kasteel Vrederic was Jacobus's granddaughter Rietje.

In the fifth diary, the famous time-traveling family left the seventeenth century where Jacobus was buried with his beloved wife Margriete. While their granddaughter Rietje was walking back home and entered the Kasteel Vrederic courtyard, some soldiers betrayed her and entered the courtyard of the castle. Alexander, Rietje's husband and a seventeenth-century knight was walking back from the second floor as one goon shot toward Rietje. All Ahana heard was the last surviving heir of the castle will be gone. Jacobus's family lineage will be gone and Alexander had promised he would keep her alive and have more family lineage to continue the family tree.

Ahana thought quickly as she stood in between the frozen Rietje and the gun. Ahana bled to death on the floors of the castle as she tried to save the last heiress of Kasteel Vrederic with her own life.

Today through the door of reincarnation, the Kasteel Vrederic family members have returned in the twenty-first century. Different diaries have been added to their library as Erasmus van Phillip and Anadhi Newhouse van Phillip, the parents of Jacobus van Vrederic, returned in *Be My Destiny* in the twenty-first century. It is their union that brought back their famous diarist son as Dr. Jacobus Vrederic van Phillip through the door of reincarnation. His cousins too joined him as his adopted brothers, Antonius van Phillip and Andries van Phillip. The very close-knit family members all live in a joint-family castle called Kasteel Vrederic.

That's how the Kasteel Vrederic series was born and continues as a paranormal family drama through diaries written and recorded in first person through different members of the Kasteel Vrederic family. Love stories, paranormal stories, and family dramas are written there. To this day, we have seven diaries written about this family which the world population have had a chance to read as a guide through history. In the world of Kasteel Vrederic, reincarnation is a blessing. Time traveling is a new path to discovery as through dreams all are united on Earth and beyond. Also, this paranormal family now has the immortality serum in the seventh diary. Here, faith is believing not questioning.

Yet even in this world, a torn page of a diary was lost. This is the story of a woman who had been fighting destiny to reunite with her beloved, dead or alive. She had been there for the Kasteel Vrederic family members as they too were there for her. Yet throughout time and through generational gaps, their connection was lost as the loose piece of paper from a diary flew away and now has landed in New York City.

Now come on and let's see if in this life, the famous Kasteel Vrederic family members return and be the guardian angels of this bruised and battered girl. Will they take her and her children under the wings of the famous family? Even if not in Naarden, the Netherlands, maybe they can spread their wings of protection to help and guide this lonely woman back to her beloved who waits for her by the Sands Point Lighthouse on the banks of the Long Island Sound, in Long Island, New York, in the United States.

Will they be able to rescue the child bride named Ahana Roy, and save her shattered wings? She was reincarnated yet what about her sailor husband, Frederic van der Bijl, who was not reincarnated? How will a ghost and a child bride unite where they must not only cross over the abuses of being a child bride, but the bride of life and dead.

This is the diary of Ahana Roy. Let's read along to find out how she will cross all of these bridges and leave a lesson for this world to never forget the tears of a child bride.

PROLOGUE:

Escaping For Love

"I became a prisoner and tolerated all the physical and emotional torture, yet when I saw your frightened face, I your mother for you my child, became the warrioress."

Thunder was roaring as lightning sparked through the windows. I am scared of the roaring storms as they remind me, I have no one to ask for help. My inner heart has hope that maybe someone will hear my cries, just maybe. During a storm, my sobbing sounds too get buried like I am buried alive. No one will arrive to help me because this is my destiny, the fate of a child bride.

It was late in the night when I heard the wall clock indicating it was late loudly in the hallway. Even during the storm, it felt like the sound was banging on my wall. I jumped out of bed in fear for I knew my daughter needed help. I had to take her to the hospital yet how would I go without being noticed? I had to acquire the courage I was lacking to save my innocent child. I knew I must rise from the ashes even though I laid in bed with my wings shattered.

The bruises on my face were dark and had not healed yet. My back hurt so much that I could not stand properly. What would I say without telling the truth? This society would never hear my stories nor would they ever understand. So, I called the only person on Earth I knew would listen to me. I called Anadhi Newhouse van Phillip for help, an author I had met while I was with my abusive husband. She is a famous dream psychic who had held my hands and told me if I ever needed help to call her. I don't know why I could only see her face as I needed someone to hold on to. The unknown, unseen vast skies were telling me to take her help. Maybe somehow I am related to her.

I rang the mysterious number I had saved in my hidden secret chest. The phone rang and an unfamiliar voice answered the phone. Hearing his voice, I wanted to hang up and run with my daughter and hide somewhere, but his voice pulled me toward him, not away from him. I wanted to ask do I know you? Who are you? Why did my inner soul say I somehow know you?

Maybe in my imaginary world where I too have a perfect family, you were there like a brother, maybe an uncle, or just a friend. If the phone could be an invisible wall, I would jump through it and fall on his chest. Who was this person and why was his voice making me feel like we had a past-life connection?

He said, "This is Jacobus Vrederic van Phillip. How may I help you?"

Again, it was either his comforting voice or it was strange to hear a voice on the other side at this time of the night. This was a male voice, and I knew I feared all male voices, but something about his voice gave me so much comfort. It felt like a warm hug from a brother or a son. I felt like screaming and asking him, "Where were you all of this time?"

Yet I only told him, "I am in danger and need Anadhi's help. She told me if I ever needed anything, to call her. It did not matter what time of the night or day it might be. She would be there for me. I need her help right now. My child might not make it through the night if I don't have someone who could help me. I am lost and I won't make it as my shattered soul needs a place or a person whom I can turn to right now."

I cried and said in Bangla, "*Amar baccha mara jabe. Anadhi kothay*? (My baby will die. Where is Anadhi?)"

The voice on the other side said clearly in Bangla and English, "*Anuroodh kori apne shanto haun.* Please calm down. She is here, and I am her son. We will be at your home within minutes, just give me your address. We will not tell any one of your family members about your call. We will say we needed your help at this odd hour so we just walked into your home for we knew you would be there for us anywhere, anytime. Dear stranger, I promise you we will be there."

The phone call ended, and I checked my young daughter as I knew her fever was not subsiding. I wondered if they were too rich to worry about a poor child bride like myself. Would they really come? Were they actually the kindhearted people I have heard of and in my secret mind, I have learned to love, at least through Anadhi's dream diaries and books on dreams?

Then after a while, I heard a doorbell. With all my might and strength, I managed to walk to the door. As I opened the door with a mountain of fear hidden within my chest, there I saw in the dark night, glowing under the moon's glorious light was Anadhi with her whole family. The famous Kasteel Vrederic family members were at my door. I read about them and knew somehow my heart kept calling their names.

I hugged my dear friend of only a few minutes' acquaintance. I told her, "I am a child bride living with fear. My child is sick and I can't take her to the hospital. I was beaten up by my husband. He beats me and my child always. This is my only child. My daughter is young and questioned my husband why he was hurting me. So, she too got injured. I told her to not get involved but I guess at her age, she can't differentiate domestic violence from a normal couple's arguments."

Then I saw a male about six feet tall, maybe around thirty years old with brown hair come forward and ask me, "Are you pregnant? How many months are you and why are you in pain?"

I saw him walk inside with a woman by his side. I watched both of them and for no known reason, I jumped in their midst and started to cry. I hugged them both as if I had not seen them for so long and finally had seen them, maybe after thousands of years. I realized it all seemed strange but they never said anything and hugged me back. After I realized how awkward it seemed, I jumped backward.

I watched his kind eyes and replied, "I think I'm about six months pregnant, but I'm not sure. My daughter and I both were beaten by my husband. If I utter this to anyone, he will make sure I don't see my daughter or my unborn child ever again. He will send me back to my home country without my children and with the shame and disgrace of being called a divorced woman. Then, my parents, the ones who bought me from my birth parents, would kick me out and I might even be killed. In my country, divorced women are disgraced and families consider them better dead than alive."

Everyone watched me not with tears but with complete understanding and anger as Anadhi's husband Erasmus, whom I met only once then said, "You will come with us to our home. You will not be known as the child bride but the woman who fought back. I will make sure this world never again sends girls out to be wedded and thrown into the hands of predators as prey ever again."

I was bleeding very hard and knew I might lose my unborn child at the hands of a monster who only cared about young girls and how fast he could have them in his bed. He was kind and nice to me as if I was his baby girl for a long time until he showed his true face and color, in a faraway land where he brought me to, the land you all know as the city that never sleeps, New York City. Yet still it was so strange no one ever heard my screams or cries for help, as if I did not even exist until one day I bumped into a woman named Anadhi Newhouse van Phillip.

Now you my reader, do come along and take a journey through my diary, the diary of a child bride who did not hide away in shame but fought back for herself and her child. I will fight for my daughter even to my death so she does not become a child bride and never falls prey to a monster or becomes the victim of abuse like I did. Maybe one day, you the victims of the same abuse will find the courage you need on a very stormy night as you read through my diary.

This is the diary of a woman who stood up on her own feet against her family, her captors who called themselves her in-laws, and her abusive husband as she was the victim of being born into a poor family and a society which sees nothing wrong in anyone being a child bride. My birth mother had said it's my own fault I am a girl and not a boy, for if only I would have been born as a male, then my life would have been very different. I was sold to another couple for money my poor family needed to buy bread for themselves and their sons.

Yes, this is my story. I am Ahana Roy born in Bangladesh. I am a child bride and a victim of gender discrimination. Here in my diary, you will see how this society had shattered my wings, yet through my faith and belief in the unknown, and my ties to my past lives, I have risen from the ashes. This diary I have named *Shattered Wings: Diary Of A Child Bride.*

CHILD BRIDE

I am a girl
Born to a world,
Where girls have no say,
For my words remain,
Within my chest.
I smile when I am sad.
I smile when I am mad.
I smile when I am scolded at.
I smile even when I am hurt.
I ask you,
How would you know
When I am happy,
Or
When I am sad?
For I have been told
Girls should
At all times only
Smile
And never show
Any other feelings.
I got excited when
I was told

I would become a bride.
I would be wearing rich clothes,
I would have expensive shoes,
I would even get to wear makeup.
Maybe after the game ends,
I would be able to
Eat rich food,
And I wouldn't be scolded at
For trying to get
Rid of my hunger,
So I wouldn't have to weep,
And hide my tears,
For my stomach
Knows not
When to not ask for food.
I would then smile not in fear,
But in joy.
Yet the day passed by quickly,
As I was brought to the house
Of an elderly man,
Who had pretended,
To be my groom,
During our make-believe
Play.

Yet now the play was over,

So, I wanted to go home

Back to my mother's lap,

Who I left home was crying,

For me.

She had said she wished I was a boy,

Yet I told her I loved being a girl,

For now I could put makeup

On like my dolls,

For my make-believe play.

I was upset what if she gets sick.

I needed to run away.

Yet it was then in one night,

I became an adult

After I was forcefully

Converted to become a bride

Of a monster.

My tears did not stop,

Nor did my pain.

For I did realize,

Going to bed hungry

Was far better than

Being in bed with a monster.

I watched the young boys

Of my age watch me,

And make fun of me

As their parents were

Making sure

Their boys would

Grow up to be

Educated adults.

I wished upon a star tonight

If only time could be reversed,

And

My life could be different.

If only I could be born

As a boy,

For then I would not have been

A

CHILD BRIDE.

CHAPTER ONE:

New York City

"The lights never go dim, nor are the paths ever bare, yet no one hears my cries, nor do they see my tears or pain as they don't see the truth but only what they want to see."

The city of dreams, New York City, is famous for its tall buildings. I wondered how they were all lighted if I could not see any lanterns lighting them. I wondered how these buildings were so tall as if they could touch the skies. My small village in Bangladesh had no tall buildings.

I had gone to the capital city Dhaka for the first time as I turned three years old. There were rickshaws and autorickshaws everywhere. The cars were so loud and honking as if they wanted to awaken every sleeping soul. Big buses and huge trucks scared my inner soul. So many people crowded the streets. I wondered if all the people from around the whole Earth had just landed there. The air seemed so cloudy yet not with fog but some kind of smoke. Somehow I felt good, like maybe I could run away with my little feet somewhere there. I wouldn't eat much and didn't need to have fancy clothes. I was used to walking barefoot. If only I could hide someplace in this big city.

I was brought to a magical home that was so tall. I wondered how they had built it. There was no tin roof and no mud holding the house up. This house almost reached the sky. All the tall buildings and the lights looked magical. The cars and buses were running without any cows pulling them. The city was like a treasure island where I got to have all the food I could not even dream about. I was gifted silk dresses and new shoes by this family. They gave me all the things I could ever dream about. I was told they were my in-laws as my mother sold me to them for money. I never saw a husband even though my mother said I was going to play a marriage game and I would be the bride.

This new family raised me for a few years and let me learn English. They taught me how to act with rich kids. I found out my parents sold me to them for ten thousand Bangladeshi taka. I loved my new family as they were always nice with me and all the other girls who resided in their home. They said they like raising young girls and that's their way of helping a society where girls are not loved or desired at birth.

I forgot what my mother looked like or other members of my family. I was happy here as I got to eat and sleep in a luxurious bed. My mother used to beat me up for saying I was hungry. Here though I could tell everyone I was hungry without being afraid. Yet my life changed as I met my husband for the first time when I turned nine years old.

My adoptive parents had told me they were my in-laws. They were the only parents I knew, so I trusted them more than I trusted my own life or my birth family. Yet I didn't know why I wouldn't see my sisters who were being brought up by them as soon as the girls would have their periods. A sister named Malina had told me not to let them know about my period, as then I would regret my life eternally.

Financial circumstances had made girls a burden for some families while some families made money by selling girls to the highest bidders as soon as the girls had started to have their periods. So, we were brought up to believe we were all family until we in the eyes of our caregivers became adults.

I did share the news of my period and had learned to regret the day ever since. For after that day, I have only faded memories of how I had accompanied a white gentleman who had blond hair and blue eyes, about forty years old, to New York City. I held his hands as I thought he was Superman whom I had seen on the television set where this guy flies and comes to rescue people in distress.

Yet my Superman turned out to be Lex Luther the villain, not the hero. I had stayed with him as his bride in the world's greatest city. I stayed hidden in his huge townhouse near Fifth Avenue in Manhattan for a few years. The streetlights and the outside sounds had been my company for years. I never played with girls as my childhood was robbed by my husband and my family members, because I was born into a poor family.

No one knew I was the wife of a middle-aged man, until I had my daughter. I had shared the house with three other women who were his wives yet they too had no voice. Each one was sent back to their home countries in Pakistan, India, and Nepal. My husband told me he does not like older women, so he sends them back home as soon as they become too old for him.

None of the girls were allowed to take legal status in the United States as they were sent back. I assumed the girls were being brought into the country as household helpers or as nannies of a very wealthy man. Yet this man had no children, only his child brides, until I had my daughter and changed his life forever.

After living with my violent husband for a few years, I became too old for him when I turned eighteen years old. My daughter was sickly from birth and turned three years old today. All three years of her life witnessed abuse and horror that haunts her to sleep every night. Three years ago at the age of fifteen, I had stood near a New York subway station trying to run away with my newborn daughter, I ran into a young woman. I bumped into her as she stopped me and felt my child. I thought there in the skies was lightning that had shown some light in front of me. I stopped as I saw out of the lightning appeared a woman.

She asked me, "Hey where are you going? Watch your step. You could have fallen and dropped the sleeping child. The baby seems hot to the touch, is she all right?"

I watched her in fear as I told her in Bangla and Hindi, "*Apni Bangla bollen? Aapko Hindi aati hai?* (Do you speak Bangla? Do you speak Hindi?) How did you jump out of the lightning?"

She replied in English, "Yes, I do speak both. Why do you ask? Are you all right? Who is this baby girl? Did you bang your head or something because I was standing here for a while? What lightning are you talking about? Is she your sister? Where are your parents? Also, let me take you home. The child seems to be sick and needs attention. I am a mother and mother-in-law of two doctors and I can help you."

At that time, the stranger saw my face and she recognized the signs of abuse very quickly. She observed me very cautiously.

I met Anadhi that one cold shivering night. She was kind and carried my newborn baby girl. She did not realize I was trying to run away nor did she know I was the child's mother. Who would have thought I had my daughter at the age of fifteen?

I could not lie to the kind woman, so I told her, "I am Ahana and this is Hana my daughter. I am a child bride. My parents sold me to a monster who is very powerful and I have no way of going anywhere for then I would lose my child."

I had cried and told her, "I must stay with him for the sake of my daughter. He will take her away from me if he finds out I am trying to run away from him."

Anadhi gave me a card and told me, "Come with me if you trust me. My family members will all be here soon and I know my husband Erasmus can help you. Please let us help you. I promise I won't tell anyone or get you into any problem."

It was then my monster custodian came walking like a very rich and famous person. He came near me and said, "I see you have my child with you. I was searching everywhere for her. Are you trying to run away with my daughter? If so, I will call the police. You are here as her caregiver, not so you can take my child away from me. Anyone who sees you will know you can't be her mother. You have brown skin, black hair, and brown eyes, and my daughter has white complexion with blonde hair and blue eyes, like me."

I could say nothing as he had the police follow up and come take me with them. I watched Anadhi stare back at me as I felt she knew I was saying the truth.

She, however, shouted at Mr. Hunter, my husband, as she said, "I have brown skin, yet my father was white and my mother was from India. My sons are all white as their father, my husband, standing next to me is a white Dutchman. I am sure you must know of a lot of inter-racial marriages and children in New York City."

Mr. Hunter said nothing nor did he acknowledge Anadhi. I said nothing as how could I walk away from my monster husband when all the laws of this land and people were all blind to the truth and only saw me as a predator and my monster husband as an innocent victim?

I only worried why life had given me so much misery and then made me the predator, not the victim. I wanted to scream and tell all I never kidnapped anyone, neither am I the nanny as this child is my own child. I had given birth at home, so there could be no records of me being her mother.

I spilled tears and let Anadhi see my tears, if only tears were words. She did understand as she waved her hands and whispered in my ears, "I believe you. When you too believe in yourself, do give me a call. I know you speak of the truth. I know this is your child and I will break Earth and

Heaven to make sure this world too knows she is your child. I will be back as I will fight for you even if you don't fight for yourself."

I watched Anadhi's husband talk with the police and the police left me with my abusive and elderly husband. I didn't know what Erasmus told them but they left me alone and never even questioned me. I watched my abusive husband talk with them and tell them I was the child's nanny.

He screamed in front of everyone and said, "I gave you a home and I have been providing for your whole damn family for all these years. If you ever do any such thing ever again, I will have you sent back home. Your whole family will be homeless and on the streets."

I wondered why the police never asked me why I was with him alone. I am underage and how was it I was allowed to be with a man all by myself. I realized my husband must have lied about my age. Anadhi watched me as I was forced into the car of my abusive husband.

After all this time, tonight my prayers were answered. I turned eighteen and my daughter three. I had to call Anadhi for help. I had kept her card safely hidden all of this time. I wondered why Anadhi never got in touch with me. Yet I knew she must have had her own troubles as she came from a foreign land. My small life experiences had given me enough courage to help my child and myself. I gained enough courage to run away from my home with my child and call her for help. I knew I had taken the first step to a great struggle ahead of myself. I walked out from the only life I had known that was normal all my life, except when my normal life hurt my child. The physical pain I had hidden under my tolerance yet the emotional pain was unbearable.

I knew I must do something for my daughter or else she too would end up a child bride like I did as her monster father only knew abuse and his own sexual desires. He had brought young girls from abroad and sold them to elderly men like himself. These girls were at times sold all over the world. Sex trafficking got him the financial freedom he needed. My husband repeatedly tried to rape my daughter. I had pulled her away from him every time and I told him I would kill both of us and our child if he tried to ever touch her. He laughed and mocked me and dared me to do it.

Nothing mattered to him more than having another child bride, or being a sugar daddy, or trafficking young girls for sex. His business was booming. He had warned all of his own child brides or sugar babies, he enjoyed his girls very young and when I turn old, I wouldn't be his favorite wife. He would send me away as a sex trophy abroad. He threatened me to allow him to have sex with my daughter or else he would have both of us killed. If he can have sex with her, then we would live happily under his roof.

I feared his threats and was scared of all the men who visit his estates. He has an island where he takes men to pick and choose their own trophy girls. I feared turning old yet I could not wait to be older as I knew then I would not be in danger but I would be the biggest danger for him. I would be the danger he brought onto himself. I needed to be brave so I could be there for my daughter and my unborn child. I knew I was carrying a girl which in societies like my own was a curse, yet I would somehow bring her up as a blessing. I had to run away before he succeeded in raping my child.

I ran out with Dr. Jacobus and his family members as they came and knocked on the door of my husband's house. They just walked in and picked up my daughter and me and walked out of the house. My abusive husband had his red angry face quiet and said nothing. I watched Erasmus watch him and with his hand gestured to my husband to be quiet and not say anything.

Anadhi told me, "Don't fear the danger but become the danger even the predator fears. We will take you and the child with us as we are your financial caregivers. We have the court orders with us. Your husband is now your ex-husband as we have legal papers. He won't say anything as he will be busy defending himself from the crimes he has been committing. He won't be charged for marrying you as your parents gave you away, but he will be facing other charges such as sex trafficking and as a pedophile as he tried to touch his own daughter."

I prayed for the first time in my life. I learned to become a Christian by watching television. I didn't know what religion I belonged to as I was sold as a child to a non-religious family. I asked my Lord to protect my child and let her not ever know or see the life her mother had lived. I watched the busy New York City from the hospital room and asked my Lord to keep all little princesses safe and protected within their parents' embrace. I prayed in this big busy city where dreams filled with hope of freedom from all obstacles do come true as this is the greatest city in the world. New York does have a law which protects child brides. I wondered if this city could protect a single lonely woman and her daughter from the hands of an international criminal.

From the hospital windows, I watched the busy streets of a famous city. I could hear in my mind the famous song, "Downtown," yet I still felt lonely in the big and vast place we all call New York City.

NEW YORK CITY

Stay with the people.

Be amongst the crowd,

For then, when or if ever

One finds herself

In trouble,

Or lost,

Someone,

Or another,

Will be there,

For you.

Yet I screamed.

I cried.

I whimpered

As I

Was raped.

I was abused.

I was kept

As a

Captive prisoner

In my own house,

As I am

Known to you and

To all,

As

The child bride

Whom no one,

Hears,

Nor sees,

As I am

A burden

For you

And the society,

Where no one

Listens,

Or understands

The cries

Of a child bride

Who lives not

In seclusion.

Nor am I kept

On an island,

Yet here I am

Living amongst

All of you,

In the city you know as

The Big Apple,

And its name is
NEW YORK CITY.

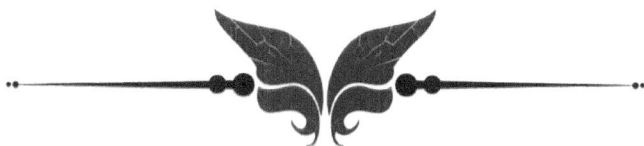

CHAPTER TWO:

Guided By Dreams

"Dreams are messages from the beyond, which I never believed in until they became my only guiding lights."

The cold big hospital building filled with so many people felt very lonely. I was freezing in fear as I waited for any news of my daughter eagerly. Covered under a heavy blanket on a hospital bed, I waited for my daughter's results to come in, I was thinking about my steps forward. As I closed my eyes, I saw him again, a man calling me from the foggy skies. Every time I fell down and needed some kind of help, this man would come to me in my dreams. He would guide me in ways I could never explain to anyone on this Earth.

I wondered when had I fallen asleep? I so wished he would keep on coming to only help me. Yet I never thought who he was and why I was never afraid of this stranger. Somehow, he came back to me even in this cold hospital bed.

He said, "Sweetheart, are you all right? Have you walked out of danger? Did you take your child with you, or did he force her to stay? Remember, you must run away from him and never ever be alone with him again. Also, keep your daughter far away from him. Somehow, try to find the Vrederic family members if that's still their surname. I believe it's different now so please connect the lines and find them."

Like a real Earthly man, he was walking around somewhere in his house. He was so calm but worried for me.

I feared men so much yet I knew I could trust my dream man. As a child, I had seen him. He would ask me to be brave and not cry. He promised he would come and get me, but he never came in real life.

I waited by the windows hoping he would fall from the skies and be there for me. My childhood was gone from my life as a storm had come to my life and had wiped out all the visibilities of childhood. I started to call him my dream man. He remained my secret, my sanctuary where I could escape to whenever I needed him. I just had to hope he would come into my dreams for there were times I had gone for days without ever seeing him.

He did somehow show up in my dreams, when I least expected him. Sometimes like a cloud to protect me from burning myself out. Sometimes like a ray of sunshine as I stood frozen in fear. I realized he was the only reason I had survived through all the obstacles of life. Maybe he was an angel who was guiding me from the beyond. Yet I had always hoped he would be coming to my door somehow, where he would just take me under his wings and keep me safe eternally there. I could fly away with him like the rising phoenix. We could both rise from the ashes and be reborn together to experience love together in a new life.

Tonight he told me, "If the Kasteel Vrederic family asks you, then do go with them. Don't hesitate. Let them help you. You need to be with a family who can help and protect you and maybe other girls who too need to be rescued. I will find you as I find the Kasteel Vrederic family. Maybe it's hard for you to believe but I feel like I am in a different time zone than you are. So maybe Anadhi, daughter-in-law of Kasteel Vrederic, can help. I met her once when she had traveled to the seventeenth century. There was a war going on and I had known Rietje, their ancestor, very well. I am first cousin to Alexander, the warrior, who is the husband of this great warrioress. He had solely fought and protected the great family home which you today know as Kasteel Vrederic. Find Rietje. She will be able to guide you to me."

That's when my sleep broke and I watched Jacobus walk in with Margriete, his wife, who is a pediatric heart surgeon. I wanted to jump out of bed and hug them both. I didn't know why I felt like I too knew them in a different place or a different time.

Margriete watched me for a while as she patted my daughter. She kissed my child's head and said, "She will be just fine. Yet I won't go around the bush but will tell you directly, we need to have her in surgery soon. I don't know if you understand or follow me but your child has a heart murmur. She was probably born with it."

I listened to them and started to cry in Bangla as I told them, "My English is all right. I can read and write fluently, but I can't speak very fluently. I just need to know if my daughter is dying or if she will live."

Anadhi was there as were her husband and son Jacobus whom I trusted with all my being. They fought with the law enforcement and had brought lawyers to my house. They had rescued my daughter and me from the monster. Yet the monster said they had not seen the last of him as he would sue all of us and they would have a lawsuit against them.

Somehow Jacobus had already testified as a doctor that my ex-husband was abusing me and had tried to rape my daughter and other young girls rescued from the same house. I was not even aware how they did this all so fast. Yet I realized they were investigating my monster ex-husband for all this time since I had bumped into Anadhi.

Erasmus told him, "Bring it on as you will realize you just found yourself a challenge you would have thought you never got into."

Then Erasmus told me they have been keeping an eye out for me all of this time and had never left me alone. I knew Erasmus was Jacobus's father and my friend Anadhi's husband. I realized somehow they too realized we had a connection from the beyond.

It was late as we brought my child to the hospital and where she was fighting for her life. I knew something was wrong as she always fell ill very quickly and was always out of breath and tired. I knew if anyone could help her, it was this family. They were here for me without even asking any questions. I knew they lived in a faraway country as they were visiting doctors performing heart surgeries in this very special hospital.

I told Margriete, "Dear Margriete, please take my child into your own hands. From today, she is your responsibility. You probably know this is a mother's worst nightmare. Yet I believe in my nightmare, I have found my blessed angels, the Van Phillip family members. I am assuming you all are known as the Kasteel Vrederic family."

Margriete held my daughter in her chest and said, "I am a mother who had lost her daughter and was lucky to have her back as my niece. Yes, I know how it feels. I promise you will never see me just as a doctor but as a friend, and your daughter too, will be my niece, not just a child. All children of this world I see as my own children. That's why I am a doctor and so is my husband Jacobus. We will both do our best and only do as I would do for our own child."

I waited with Anadhi and Erasmus as my daughter went through her first heart surgery that night. I wondered why do innocent people have to suffer so much? My heartless ex-husband went on making people suffer while he himself did not even suffer or flinch.

I wished all the bad on him tonight yet I heard Anadhi say, "No, don't ever wish bad on anyone. Let karma take its own course. Your ex-husband signed the divorce papers, so tonight, you are free. Erasmus also told him if he does not give you full custody of the child, then we would bring in charges against him as a child molester with child endangerment charges."

Anadhi was silent for a while and then she held me in her arms as she said, "You will be free from him but we will need you to testify against him. You will need to be ready to get into a war with him and all the men who are forcing little girls to be child brides, sugar babies, or sex-trafficking victims. Remember in New York City, today you are safe because another woman fought a hard battle and won. You too will win here and abroad as our fight will continue beyond the borders."

I saw how Anadhi kept her emotions at bay. When she was upset or was feeling anger, she watched Erasmus and he with a wink of his eyes told her everything will be just all right. I found so much comfort in both of them. I felt like I found my parents in them today. At least from tonight, I would imagine them as my parents when I needed comfort. I watched Anadhi as she was looking at me. She smiled and hugged me in her embrace.

I watched Anadhi and told her, "I have both of you now. I will do my share and I hope I am the last child bride on this Earth. Yet in my dreams, I have been guided by a man who has asked me to find a brave warrioress. I will let you know her name when I find her, for I know you believe in dreams."

Anadhi watched me and said, "I must go back to the hotel as my granddaughters are waiting there with my other sons. I always put my granddaughters to bed as that's my promise to them, and each night we the family members tell them a story and tonight is my turn. I promise I will be back soon and go over your dream with you. Until then, why don't you write your dream down in a notebook? Also when we finally are back from Egypt as we must be there soon, I would love to share story time with your daughter and the unborn child like I do with my granddaughters."

I watched the kind woman running out to be with her family and admired her so much for being such a kind soul. I wished this Earth could give us more people like Anadhi. I wrote down the name of a woman I had never met, named Rietje. Somehow, she was involved in the Dutch Eighty Years' War. I wondered what she would say about the modern-day woman. What would she call me? A child bride? Or maybe a loser who even in this time and era can't seem to help myself from being a child bride.

I didn't get a chance to think about all of this as a policeman came into my room. He was tall and very kind looking. He said, "Are you Ahana Roy? We must let you know your house, the one you shared with your ex-husband, has been raided by the police and is now a crime spot. It is the site of criminal activities. We have unfortunately lost the predator. Even though your ex-husband has escaped, his child brides, sex-trafficking victims, drugs, and illegal guns have been found and will be placed in a safe place under police protection. You will be given complete protection until we catch him."

The policeman watched me for a while as he walked back and forth and then said, "We will need you to testify against him. Also, we believe he has numerous houses around the country where he keeps very young girls. He has a resort on an island where he keeps young girls. Why did he marry you when he did not marry others? I hope you know your marriage to him could not be legalized and will be annulled because he is married to another woman who is actually his wife of twenty-five years. She lives a few houses down from where you had lived."

I listened to him and wondered why I had no clue about the world I lived in. I had no clue the monster was married. I felt good I was free from him. I was brought here as a child and had been living in his basement for all this time. Never did I think of escaping as he would have ruined my family members, those who had sold me to this monster.

I told the policeman, "I believe he marries all the girls he brings from countries where families sell their daughters at a young age as child brides. The husband then promises to take care of the bride's family members. It's a source of income for the families. I have met three girls and they too were in the same situation I was in, except they didn't get pregnant as he had their tubes tied. I was too young to get the surgery so he made a mistake and I got pregnant. I never knew he had a wife or what kind of life he lived outside of that house. We were always kept locked up in the basement of the house. We had a television set and had phones but never did any one of us dare to call outside. I made the first call when I dialed Anadhi for help."

The policeman asked again as he watched me for a while, "Will you be brave enough to testify against him? I know you tried to run away and save your child once before but got caught by him. He told the police you were the child's nanny and it's on us as we never looked into your side of the story. I have been told the Van Phillip family will be your caregiver and they have taken all of your financial responsibilities. Just try to get better and give your daughter a big hug from all of us. We will not fail you again. Aside from the Van Phillip family, do you have any family members you would like us to contact for you?"

It was then I saw Jacobus standing at the open doorway of the hospital room. He smiled so nicely that my inner heart just melted and I knew I could trust him above all men on this Earth. I started to cry when he walked in. He walked in so calmly as he placed his hands on my head.

Jacobus said, "Yes, she does have family members who will take her in their home. Actually, my mother is her aunt and I am her cousin. I will personally take in Ahana and her daughter into our home in Sands Point. We have a house there by the lighthouse. If any other woman or girl needs a room or place to stay, we would like to open our home to all of them. Let's call this Vrederic Shelter where girls and women will always find a home for them when they need it."

The policeman then watched me as he had a lot of papers for me to sign. Margriete walked in with an American doctor who introduced himself as Dr. Johnathan Anderson.

He said, "Dr. Jacobus and his family members are visiting doctors and philanthropists. They live in the Netherlands, but they have places around the world as shelters and homes for themselves which they also open for others in need. I would like Margriete to go over the papers with you and sign them as that's what would be in your best interest. You are so lucky you have Dr. Jacobus Vrederic van Phillip, the world's best renowned cardiologist and a very special doctor, personally operating on your daughter."

The policeman left as I was taken to the children's wing where my daughter was recovering from her surgery. There I saw a tall woman who looked Italian. She was sitting with my child, singing a sweet song, and patting my daughter's hair.

I walked in as she said, "I am Katelijne and I am Anadhi's daughter-in-law. My husband is Antonius van Phillip and the woman who is opening the window is Tara Bella, another daughter-in-law of this Van Phillip family. Her husband is Andries van Phillip. We were on our way to Egypt when we were diverted to New York as Big Brother Jacobus and his wife Margriete had to perform an emergency surgery. So it happens, we were all in town when you had rung the phone."

Tara Bella then asked, "May I have her now?"

She took my three-year-old daughter in her arms. My daughter had been crying ever since her surgery and refused to stop crying. Yet as she went into Tara Bella's arms, she stopped crying. Tara Bella was singing a Bengali song as she held my daughter in her arms. I tried to listen to her and understood what she sang. I sang with her.

She sang, "*Jodi tor dak shune keo na ashe tobe ekla cholo re* (if no one comes even after you call them then walk alone)."

I asked her, "You know Bangla?"

She kissed Hana on her cheeks and her chest as she then said, "My memories are not very good. Once upon a time, I had known Bengali and my Big Mama Anadhi sings in Hindi, Bengali, English, and Dutch to all of the children in our home. So, we actually all picked up these Rabindranath Tagore songs from her."

Hana then said, "Mama."

I wondered why she was saying Mama when she always called me Mom. I watched the three women who seemed like my best friends. Katelijne, Tara Bella, and Margriete all looked like movie stars standing in my room. I wondered how Anadhi was their mother-in-law as they all look the same age. Margriete was treating my daughter who was awake and talking to everyone. They all looked like a family. I felt some kind of comfort in my inner soul. I felt like I would safely call my future to rise from the ashes. Maybe some kind of premonition. Hana kept on calling Tara Bella "Mama" and I had no clue why.

I heard Katelijne tell Hana, "Do you know Jacobus and Margriete were and are still are my doctors? I love having them as my doctors because they healed me completely. Now I don't get tired all the time. I also have a daughter and a niece whom I can take care of without any trouble. I have special permission to bring my daughter in here to meet you. She is roughly about your age I believe. She will be here soon with her cousin and their two friends. Won't you too be my niece forever?"

Hana watched the woman who was busy with her and said, "Yes, Aunty Katelijne! I would love it as I would love my Mama Tara Bella!"

Then I saw she kissed Tara Bella, and kissed my head as she said, "Hi Mom."

I sat next to my child as I was tired and knew I would be going into labor soon. I had to wait a few more weeks before I could deliver. I wondered if I should tell Margriete

I started to have spotting. That's when I watched a child come into the room with a big basket of bread.

She walked in and said, "Hello there! I am Griet and I have a basket of fresh bread for you."

I hugged the child and thought she was the most amazing child I had ever laid my eyes on. As she walked in with Anadhi, I knew they were Kasteel Vrederic family members. She had with her another child who jumped on top of Jacobus and hugged him.

Both girls had with them two boys who also just watched me and said nothing. Then, I watched two men walk in who I assumed were Jacobus's brothers and Anadhi's sons. They were talking with Erasmus and called him Big Papa.

The child who walked in with Griet came near me and said, "Strange face. I feel like I know you so well. You look so similar to the nurse who had helped Opa and Oma when Opa was dying last time in the seventeenth century. Are you Ahana the nurse who had risked her life and her husband's life as you two had made sure I lived when our home was under siege? You had passed away in the war and your husband swore he would wait for you throughout centuries."

I watched the young child talk about my dreams. It hurt so much. I thought maybe my dreams were in the future and I would have an opportunity to meet my dream man as the events had not happened yet. Now it seems like they did happen in the past, not the future. So, my dream man and I would have a bridge between us called time or death.

I touched her hands and said, "Rietje, the famous diarist's granddaughter. Yes, I do remember. My dream man who visits me during my time of need told me I would meet you again. I thought you were much older, not this young."

Jacobus came close to me and said, "She is young, yet she is wise and, in this life, she is not my granddaughter but my daughter. Her mother Griet is now my niece. I am the diarist you helped and for you, I have returned from the same family tree. Your stories had gone missing in my diaries as my past-life memories were scattered. I do remember you and your stories, yet I have no recollection of our last meeting as I was unconscious. You had with your life taken care of my family members. For you, my family exists to this day. Through us, your family too will continue. We will take care of you and your children, for that's our vow from the beyond."

I cried and knew I was actually back with my real family members. Those members whom I was not related through blood but through a bond that will not break even at death. Tara Bella had taken my permission to feel my womb before she left. She said a prayer for the child and me as she hugged me and my unborn child before she left.

That night, I saw my dream man again. He was smiling as he said, "I know you are with your real family members. Believe in miracles my darling, for I too will be there through the door of miracles. Like you, I too will cross the bridge of time and be in your time zone through the blessed miracles of a child the world knows as the girl with the lantern, Griet. She was Rietje's mother whom we never met for she was a spirit in the seventeenth century. I know she will be with her daughter as a sister, cousin, or a friend somehow, some way. Maybe she will also help your children who will need her through this life."

I woke up as I greeted another dawn and was happy I made it to another day. I watched my daughter sleep in our new temporary home in Sands Point, New York. Jacobus had promised me I would be taken home to Naarden, the Netherlands as soon as he could get our papers ready. My heart told me my beloved dream man was waiting there for me. I wanted to ask little Rietje and Jacobus what else they knew about him. Yet I was told by Anadhi not to rush memories from another lifetime. I should let memories come to me slowly.

For now, I must walk on my own feet and make sure my daughter and my unborn child never become a child bride. The walls of the rich and famous are always kept closed to the needy and helpless. Yet like the Van Phillip family members, there are people left on this Earth who help and hold on to the hands of the needy and the poor. I will survive as I have the Kasteel Vrederic family guiding me from far away as they all left me alone in their cottage, not far from Manhattan in New York. I will be guided by dreams.

GUIDED BY DREAMS

Through your words,

I found myself.

Waited all day

To only

See you

Once again.

Like a fog,

You come,

Yet at dawn,

You disappear like the

Morning mist.

All my pain,

All my sufferings,

I forget

When I see you.

For in front

Of only you,

I don't hide my,

Physical

Or emotional

Pain.

I know even when

No one believes,

Or sees,

Or hears

My untold

Story,

You come and

You listen,

And hear,

And you see my

Pain,

As you and

I belong together

In the land

Of dreams,

Even if not in

The land of the

Humans.

So my beloved,

Don't ever

Stay away

From me

As I wait

For you,

Always,

To be held,
To be protected
From all the monsters
Of this world,
As I know during the
Worst,
And during the best
Of times,
Through you,
My beloved,
I will survive as
I am forever
GUIDED BY DREAMS.

CHAPTER THREE:

Sands Point

"A lighthouse guides all the lost travelers back to shore yet what guides all lost twin flames back to one another?"

T he heartbeats of a child actually keep a mother alive. I felt the heartbeats of my daughter as I touched her chest with one of my hands and with the other, I felt my other daughter's heartbeats in my womb. All night, we were in a small cottage near the Sands Point Lighthouse. This cottage belonged to Erasmus and his family members.

It was a stone cottage with a huge fireplace. The porch had climbing clematis, Virginia creepers, and American wisteria blooming all over it. The cottage was furnished with all white and blue colors. The kitchen was furnished with old antique furniture. I could see Anadhi decorating this as it felt so comfortable like her.

There was a lot of acreage here where they come and stay when in the United States. There was a huge Georgian mansion on the property. The complex also had small guest cottages for invited guests. There was an orchard with apple trees. I was honored they let me stay here with my child for as long as I needed to be here. I would find a way to stand on my own feet as I had help from an unknown kind family who had placed their blessed hands on my head and were guiding me. Even though they had to leave and go to Egypt, they were with me through their kindness.

I told Anadhi as she insisted that I travel with them, "No, I must stay back here and fight for my two children. If I run away with you all, I will always feel like a loser who could never fight for herself. I want to testify against my ex-husband and let the world know I was a child bride. I am not his child's nanny but the mother of Hana and the unborn child I carry. If I go with you guys, the attorneys are saying I will lose my children to him."

I watched my friend Anadhi and her whole family so intensely worried about me that I felt guilty and thought maybe I should try to go with them. That's what even my dream man had told me. But I knew I had to fight for my children and I knew if I lost them even temporarily, I would never see my daughter ever again. She would be sent away somewhere on this Earth as a child bride or a sex worker.

Erasmus told me then, "I will give you my protection if you come with us to the Netherlands. I can't give you much protection if you stay in the United States. Anadhi's Aunt Agatha moved from Seattle and lives here as does her husband James Brown in one of our small cottages. The Browns are very old but have promised to be here soon and will help you with the transition. They travel a lot but live here mostly. They are both dream psychics and have a touch of miraculous healing powers in them. Aunt Agatha is a nurse and even at this old age, she still is at her job and works as a part-time nurse. I know you are worried about sex traffickers and others. I have spoken to the local police and the attorneys have been all warned. They will all keep an eye out for you like their own family member."

He took a breath for a while and then I watched him look at the door. We saw Jacobus come in with a lot of shopping bags as he and Margriete placed them in the house. The whole family was busy getting the cottage ready for us. I knew they were all worried for us and I wanted them to know I would be all right as I was free from the biggest obstacle of my life, my captor.

No words came to my mind as I saw then at the door was standing a man whom I never saw or knew as he stood there and said, "Jacobus, are you guys staying here for a while or leaving? I can't believe I am actually seeing you again."

No one replied to him or said anything as if no one saw him. He was wearing a sailor's clothing. I thought he looked like a person who was returning home from war.

Anadhi then said, "I felt a sudden breeze, as if someone just walked in. Jacobus, are you positive there are no ghosts here? I have always thought there was a young man who had come here. I felt like he knew you or talked to you as if he was your buddy or had known you from sometime or somewhere."

Jacobus walked over to me and he looked at the doors and the porch outside of the house. He came back and kissed his mother's head and said, "If there is a man who you have seen or heard for so many years revisiting, then Ahana would be just all right. If he is my buddy, he will take good care of Ahana. Just maybe, I chose him for Ahana in some other life. The ghost sailor would keep her safe I am positive. Besides, Aunt Agatha is coming and I know she would never leave Ahana in danger, nor would I."

I then saw my Van Phillip family members had left me alone in this amazing cottage. The home was filled with fresh groceries, medication, and all the luxuries of life. I was also provided a doctor who came and visited me every day, and my personal nurse was Aunt Agatha who lived in the cottage next to mine on the same property. I did see my sailor man come back and just stand at the corner of my room or sit on the balcony every evening. I knew he was my dream man as he too knew who I was. He left a note on my desk which read:

"Dear dream girl, I know I have visited you in your dreams as now you are in front of me. Alas if I were only alive to welcome you in this Vrederic house and my heart.

Yes, this cottage belonged to my family as we were Dutch settlers. You probably would find most of my family members in Sleepy Hollow. We lived here way before Erasmus bought this home in this life. I had known Jacobus in my previous life even though he might not remember me, he actually introduced us to each other. I promise you I will be here as your protector as long as you need me. Fear not that you don't see me. Just know I can see you. I will give you complete privacy as I am a good ghost. People have seen my apparition near the lighthouse. You will hear a lot of stories my beloved, yet don't believe everything you hear as stories change through the wagon of time and the story tellers."

I did sleep well as I knew aside from knowing him all my life, I actually was not afraid of ghosts. All my life I believed not to fear the dead. I had visited so many gravesites and saw the dead were all sleeping. They even allow you to talk without being rude or interrupting. I fear the living as they are dangerous and can physically and emotionally hurt me. I saw my little precious Hana sleep like a baby. She was my strength. I would make sure my little girl has a different life than the one I was so used to.

That's when I heard a doorbell and feared the loud sound in the middle of a soundless and peaceful morning. I got up from bed and put on a robe. I tried to peek through the peep hole, but I saw no one. I wondered was it my ghost man? Or Aunt Agatha? I knew no one could enter this home without knowing the gate code or some one letting the person in. Maybe the caretaker guard let the person in.

I had groceries delivered to my home so maybe Aunt Agatha had ordered something. I opened the door without thinking twice. There was no one on the porch as I tried to see if someone was there. I wondered maybe I was imagining someone there who was not. I tried to come back to my cottage as a hand grabbed me from the back.

I knew the touch and I froze in fear. It was the worst touch of my life. There in the bright sun, I saw him. The tall man who had fair skin and blond hair. His eyes were blue and it seemed like the most fearful face of my life. I felt like someone had placed my feet into cement and I could not move at all.

It was then from outside, a huge garden broom came flying over on top of my ex-husband. He let go of me and shook off the feeling very quickly.

My little Hana screamed her lungs out like a shriek. She was so scared of her biological father hurting her again. She cried and called for Anadhi. I knew Anadhi and her family members were on their way to Egypt for a personal matter.

She kept on saying, "Mama, help!"

I knew no one would be available even if I had screamed my lungs out. There in front of my eyes stood Mr. Hunter, my ex-husband.

He walked inside and laughed a horrible laughter. He said, "Oh, your famous Dutch family are all gone I hear. So, now you and I will face one another like how we had been. You will come back with me and you will withdraw all the lawsuits against me. I will make sure my little Hana finds her groom and is taken care of, happily ever after. I have a lot of money at stake here. I will not have you tarnish my good name. You will be sent oversees to my other buyers. Also before I sell this bitch daughter, I will have her at least once."

He then pulled my hair and slapped my face as he then said, "I will have sex with you first. Then you will know how you missed me. Then, I will rape your daughter in front of you."

Again I saw a huge broom flew in from nowhere and it banged the monster on his head. I screamed for help and I tried to open the door as he had shut the door behind him. I didn't know who I could call for help. It was then a tall man came and opened the door with a bang.

He had a gun in his hands as he said, "Move out of my property or I will shoot you as an intruder who has entered and is trying to hurt my tenants. I promise you my gun will not miss you as I have the police on the phone with me."

There in front of me was standing an elderly African-American gentleman. He was big and had an authoritative and commanding look. His skin was dark brown and his black and gray hair gave him a powerful look.

I cried and said, "Uncle James, I am so scared he wants to take my Hana and me with him and sell us both. He hurt me and I am worried about my unborn child. I feel like I'm going into labor too early. I am bleeding again and am so worried."

It was then the police came in and had taken my ex-husband out of my home. They said, "Thank you James, for keeping us on the phone. We were told by Erasmus that he might be visiting and would try to hurt these two. They both look like children. It's so sad when a child has a child and has to face so much on her own. We will handle him from now on."

I tried to avoid eye contact with him, yet I looked up and saw his anger as he told me, "My group is big and there is no way you can get everyone. There are so many after you. They will find you. I have accepted their money and they will come and get you. The funniest thing is, I don't know who they are. I couldn't tell the police or anyone anything about them as I don't know where or when they will come for you and your child. Both of you belong to them. I already sold you both. My only regret is that I could not have the little bitch."

I watched the police take him away as they told me, "You won't see him for a long time as he will be spending the rest of his life behind bars for abusing a child bride, sex trafficking, and rape charges which also includes trying to rape his own child. We have his confession on tape. We have rescued a lot of young girls from his home and his warehouses where he has been keeping them. Actually ma'am, we also rescued little boys he had brought in to be sold at the markets."

They all left and again I felt like the ground under my feet had trembled and I was standing on shaking grounds.

Aunt Agatha and Uncle James had brought me and Hana to their cottage. The cottage was slightly bigger and filled with so many treasures, it actually felt like home. It had roses growing around the home. I could smell something sweet and knew they were chocolate vines. I didn't know what a home actually looks like as I never had one. Yet this place looked like something I would love to be in.

This cottage had German schmeared paint on the outer walls. There were a lot of exposed beams in the interior. I knew all of this as I was allowed to watch TV and I loved watching cottages. On the stone fireplace wall, there were portraits of the Kasteel Vrederic family members. Anadhi was standing with a younger Aunt Agatha and Uncle James. Then, there she was with the elderly couple. I saw she had not aged yet her children were older through the portraits.

My little Hana walked over with Uncle James as he showed her all the portraits on the wall.

She asked him in her baby voice, "Grumpy Gramps, where is my picture? There you have Mama and Piano Papa. Where am I and baby?"

We were all watching her as she was pointing to someone but we could not understand. Yet I watched Uncle James and Aunt Agatha watch her for a while and none of us said anything to one another.

Uncle James kissed her and said, "I don't think I understood everything you said but I am positive you just called me Grumpy Gramps. And so forever little princess, I will be your Happy Gramps."

I watched Mr. and Mrs. Brown and knew they were a blessed couple and I hoped my Lord granted them happiness forever. I prayed they didn't get any of my luck and that they would always be like this. I just found my heaven on earth in this home. This one day will be my eternal gift.

Aunt Agatha said, "Aside from the children, everyone looks similar in age in Kasteel Vrederic. They don't age after a certain number of years. There are so many portraits and so many mysteries hidden within the walls of Kasteel Vrederic and the family members, you will realize once you do visit them and read all of the diaries. Until then do know miracles are just that, miracles. Believe in them and let the power of miracles give ordinary folks like us something to hold on to. You should stay here with us until all of your troubles are over and you have given birth to this child safely."

I watched the open veranda around the cottage and saw there in front of us was a lighthouse that was standing tall and I could see the Long Island Sound. The blue water was so comforting that it felt like a warm bath for my hungry soul. I wondered was he lonely today sailing in the vast ocean all by himself when he should be with me. I knew we had a vast space in between us that no one can cross, living or dead. Yet through dreams, we can still unite. I would have him through any path available to me. Now I just saw his ghostly figure watch out for me from the vast ocean.

Aunt Agatha made eggs and toast with a fresh pot of herbal tea. She also had coffee brewing in the coffee maker. There on the table was fresh churned butter and strawberry jam. Fresh fruits were placed on a platter and fresh-squeezed orange juice. She carried Hana and placed her on a chair with a cushion for height. Then, she poured orange juice into Hana's glass. Hana was smiling and felt special as she was being treated like a princess. I knew this was the first time my little Hana actually sat on a real chair.

I felt my heart ache as I knew we had a big battle we must face lying ahead of us. Tears deceived me as they poured out of my eyes. I never had this kind of love in my life. I knew I was being given a miracle that I feared was a dream and would be gone if I had opened my eyes. Yet I so wanted this memory to be safe and secured within my inner chest eternally. I prayed if this is a dream, then I wanted this dream to never end, or to be sealed with all my love in my chest. Maybe I could keep a portrait of this moment. Uncle James had his cell phone out and took some pictures of us.

Uncle James was watching me as he said, "This is for Hana, so I can add her pictures on my wall. Ahana, I understand we all have something in common, dreams, as I imagine you believe in dreams."

I watched them both sitting at the small kitchen table as the doors were open and the fresh breeze entered the house. I thought the air was saying miracles are within reach in this house. Even if things go downhill, I felt like my dreams had come true.

I watched both kindhearted humans sitting in front of me and told them, "Yes, I do believe in dreams. I have this person who comes and visits me in my dreams. He said he is my twin flame from the past, and we will unite somehow even if time and place do not give us a chance, we will cross it and be together in life or in death. If I do die during this battle, I would want you two and the Van Phillip family to raise my children as your own."

I wiped my tears and then I told them, "If I have a short life, then I would pray the life I was not granted be given to you all so you can be there for her. I believe she too calls someone her Mama and Piano Papa. If she is ever sick, this Mama and Piano Papa somehow always appear and, in her dreams, they heal her. Sometimes I hear this Mama of

Hana sing to her. If things go wrong, please tell Hana's Mama, I just carried the children yet maybe just for her."

Uncle James watched me as tears fell from his eyes. I knew he was a dream psychic and had written a lot of books. I wanted to ask him if he knew about my future but could not get it out in words as I felt the child in my womb move. For a while, he sipped his fresh mug of coffee. I knew Aunt Agatha gave me tea as I was pregnant and she wanted me to have this herbal tea to help my nerves settle down.

Uncle James said, "A Dutchman from the seventeenth century who had eventually come to the United States as a sailor leaving his young married wife alone in the Netherlands, or had she passed away? His wife was a nurse who had tended the wounded people during the Dutch Eighty Years' War. He left everything he knew behind to forget his past and came here. He lost his wife in the war where she the healer too had become the victim. He was the sailor who never stopped looking for her even after his death. He kept on searching for her in the Atlantic Ocean and in the Pacific Ocean, until he found the tunnel of dreams. His dreams told him she was not gone but would rise again from the ashes. By the vast water, you two will meet again and maybe rise from the ashes again together."

I saw Aunt Agatha clean up the dishes and was busy baking a pie for lunch. She looked like an angel with her blonde and gray hair in a bun. I loved this couple and knew time had nothing to do in a love story as I fell in love with this couple the first time when I saw them. They will be my parents forever, the imaginary parents I always daydreamed about. Blessed I felt to be with them even for a short time. My faith in true love was not shattered by the beast as I found this happy couple.

I wondered if they had any children of their own. They both knew so much of the future yet they chose to live in the present not allowing their knowledge to take away from the present. I realized then God only gives as much as you can take, not more. That's why we the weak can't see our future.

Aunt Agatha and Uncle James must read minds as Aunt Agatha then said, "Anadhi is my child. She is my grandniece and the only surviving child our family has. She and the Kasteel Vrederic family members who are now known as the Van Phillip family are my family members. I had no children. Through Anadhi, I now have so many and I pray more will come. James and I are blessed as Anadhi, Erasmus, Jacobus, little Griet and Rietje are all either on the phone or at the door if we don't see each other for a while.

Margriete, Andries, Antonius, Katelijne, and Tara Bella all are always one phone call away."

I watched the couple look outside as somehow there was a windstorm coming from somewhere. I wondered how it felt to be outside watching a storm in real life. All my life I had stayed in the basement of my captor.

Uncle James said, "Our family members are dream psychics who also time travel and have gifts from the beyond. You must believe in him who calls you from the beyond. Yet you must not rush time or the things happening around you. For your child, we must make sure the sex traffickers and the gangs that are after you or work for your ex-husband Mr. Hunter are imprisoned or are not after you anymore as they are a very nasty and dangerous group and will stop at nothing. We must make them pay for their sins and catch them so no more innocent victims are found either dead, pregnant, or sold at the world sex bazaars."

Uncle James watched the water moving outside in the Long Island Sound as he said, "I hope we can travel around the world and maybe help poor families with needed jobs and trainings, so they don't have to sell their daughters for sex or as child brides. I hope this world treats daughters as equal to their boys and don't ever have to sell them as burdens. You are from Bangladesh where you have a woman

Prime Minister, which is a huge step forward. I believe the country will go forward and maybe become one of the leaders who will end child brides worldwide."

I walked for a while and told them, "I was in a group of girls who were all brought from Bangladesh, India, Pakistan, and Nepal. I knew there were more girls brought into his house from Niger too, yet they did not stay overnight as they were sold before the first night. There is a woman who is involved in all of this. She is very rich and is married to a sex trafficker. A girl had trusted her and then realized she was the person selling these girls. Somehow she was very close with my ex-husband. I just hope she was not his wife and was just a greedy woman."

I thought about the woman and knew she was European and did not speak much English. She traveled all over the world looking for young girls. They brought these girls as young brides and sex workers. I had seen so many during my few years with the monster. I didn't know what he exactly did as business but knew he traveled a lot.

Actually, I don't even know his full name. I never asked him as I trained myself to keep my eyes and mouth shut in front of him. When he traveled, we would have the evil woman looking after us and then it was far worse than having him rape us as she would rape all and only left me alone as I was his favorite. It was a horror movie as I feared she would touch my daughter.

I told everything to Aunt Agatha and Uncle James as they had all of my testimonies recorded and gave them to the authorities. Uncle James spoke on the phone for a while and looked worried.

He told us, "The police have said somehow Mr. Hunter has escaped from prison. They are thinking he very likely left the country and will remain hidden for a while. He will go underground, which will be safe for you as they will now keep an eye on anyone like him entering the country. The police are worried about the woman who paid his bail and afterward, helped him escape. She is very powerful and might actually be the ringleader whom he works for."

Uncle James watched us and said, "Don't worry, you will all be just all right. We will survive with honor, dignity, and courage. We will fight them with all that we have. You just make sure your unborn child and Hana are safe."

That night, I saw the lighthouse glowing in the dark. I didn't know if the lighthouse was a working lighthouse or not, yet I could swear I saw the glow of the light come on our home. It was as if it was trying to warn us of the upcoming dangers we would face.

I worried if I had placed Uncle James and Aunt Agatha's lives at risk. Yet I knew I somehow must protect them and myself at any cost even if the cost was giving up my own life doing it. I prayed to the land tonight and asked her to keep Hana and her unborn sibling and the two kind hosts safe at any cost.

That's when I watched a ghost sailor come and stand by my bed near the window. He was tall and had fair complexion with long blond hair. Even though he was a ghost, I could see he had deep blue eyes like the ocean. He also wore a medieval type of clothing that somehow made me think of a sailor man.

He was glowing in the pouring moonlight as he whispered, "I will make sure everyone is safe as I am a sailor and that's my oath. I will protect the children and make sure they end up with the Kasteel Vrederic family household even if that's the last thing or only thing I can do."

I told him, "Please find me because I am near the Sands Point Lighthouse in Sands Point."

SANDS POINT

A home,

A cottage,

Where love brews

With the

First rise

Of dawn.

I smell

Fresh brewed coffee.

I hear the

Tea pot

Whistling,

As it reminds

Me,

Breakfast is being

Made for me.

I don't have to worry

About what

I have to eat.

How will I greet

The morning,

For I know in this

Small cottage,

Love brews

In the air,

As this home

Was made

And kept

For special guests

Of special

Loved ones.

I am the special

Loved one

Who never knew

Love actually

Existed

Within

The kind

Souls of

Humans with humanity.

Yet today I found

This Earth

Had one such place

On Earth,

Where I too would be

Taken care of,

And shown I too

Belong
In a family,
Where love grows
Within all the hearts,
Of the family
Members.
A vacation house,
Or a permanent home,
A cottage to grow
Old together
With humans
Who are not related,
By blood,
Yet connected
With one another,
Through the simple word
Called love.
This all came
True for me
In a small place
Not known to me
Ever before
Yet today
I found her,

ANN MARIE RUBY

You all know her as
A place in New York city
Her given name
Is
SANDS POINT.

CHAPTER FOUR:

The Guiding Lighthouse

"Fearing the ghosts whom you can't even see, you light candles and say prayers. Yet what about the humans who hunt down humans? How do you protect yourself when the danger is not hidden but in front of you?"

The night broke out with the screaming of a very frightful child. Hana woke up screaming in fear. She was shaking and scratching everyone. I worried if she was having some kind of panic attack and started to cry with her. I knew I had to be the mother and be strong, yet I felt lonely, lost, and helpless.

Then Hana said, "Mama, it hurts! Piano Papa, the bad man hurting me. Dada wants to finish me and kill me. Cousin sisters, he is hurting me! Everyone emergency! Call Big Doctor Papa now. Man wants me to take off my underwear. He wants to hurt me. I told him not to touch me. I said no, just like you told me to say. Dada slapped me Mama. Stop him, Mama please stop him."

I woke up as did Uncle James and Aunt Agatha. I held on to my child as she cried and screamed in fear. I rocked my child and watched Aunt Agatha take her in her arms.

She asked Hana, "Did you Dada ever take off your pants and hurt you?"

Hana watched her and said, "He tried to and Mom slapped him, and she called the police. We ran away remember, and we saw Anadhi there. That's how we were safe. I told him if he hurts me I will call Anadhi. She will protect me and take me to Mama and Piano Papa, also Doctor Papa and my Best Buddy Artist Papa."

I wondered how Hana even remembered what happened when she was merely a few months old. Or maybe, she was trying to recollect what happened later on and knew from me that Anadhi would come and save us. I watched Hana grow up faster than she should have had to.

I told Aunt Agatha and Uncle James, "No I did not let him. I was raped and hurt as I was beaten and left on the floor bleeding for days. Yet I did not allow him to touch my daughter. He did not care about raping his own child. He is a monster who does not care who he is hurting as he only cares about his own self. He had brought in more young girls and I tried to save as many as I could but it was hard. I am confused, who does she call every time she needs help?"

I watched Uncle James and Aunt Agatha look at each other as they remained quiet. I took a break.

Then I told Aunt Agatha, "I was kept in a house as a prisoner. A lot of women from the Indian subcontinent come and live life in their homes as they are told this is for their safety. They don't go get groceries. They don't go out to the parks, or even get to be human beings who could think for themselves. I was a child bride who was kept as a prisoner from the get-go. Mr. Hunter had invited multi-cultural families to our house who never knew I was his child bride. All the wives whom I met seemed to be in fear or were scared like I was. No one ever talked about their personal lives. Most had gotten married from age sixteen through age eighteen. I assumed I was one of them."

I saw Aunt Agatha walk around and look very angry as she said, "What about the social service? They don't know these things? Did they ever get involved or do they not know there are so many women who don't talk about being a prisoner in their own home?"

I knew this was a topic not known to all the people around the world except the victims who are taught to believe this is a normal life. Most happen to have good marriages but at the cost of losing their own identity as the women become the shadows of the men which I would have loved to be if I had my twin flame. Yet why would my twin flame want my shadow to disappear and not even be a person? In my culture, the wife wants to be protected within the shadow of her husband, not be the prey of the predator.

The stars seemed invisible that night as Uncle James, Aunt Agatha, and I sat outside on the porch. The summer storms with very cloudy skies disguised the grounds. All around us felt like the ground of some kind of horror movie set I so wanted to watch but could only read about. Aunt

Agatha had Hana on her lap rocking so ever softly. I watched my little baby girl get comfortable with Aunt Agatha and Uncle James more and more, day by day.

I wanted to ask Aunt Agatha why my daughter Hana always calls someone Mama. I was scared to ask who she called Mama, yet I felt in my heart I knew. It was as if she had a family member she trusted, and children can see their future. I just wanted to tell my child, not to forget this Mom when you find your Mama. I saw my frightened child and knew at any cost I must protect my children.

Uncle James watched me and said, "The Sands Point Lighthouse was constructed in Long Island, New York in 1809 by Noah Mason, an American Revolutionary War veteran. The lighthouse is also known as the Mitchell Lighthouse, named after Samuel L. Mitchell. The lighthouse was sold in 1924 to a wealthy trendsetter who had built the house next to it. I believe the name was Mrs. Belmont. Ultimately, the lighthouse was sold to William Randolph Hearst. Eventually he too lost the house to a bank in 1940, as he could not pay the mortgage. It's a sad but historical story. The third-oldest lighthouse still in existence on Long Island, but the lighthouse is not in use which is sad."

I watched Uncle James take little Hana and walk with her as he kissed his wife softly on her head. I knew they had a long romantical story hidden in their past which I wish I could have known. Yet I didn't want to prey and ask anything. I guess I was suppressed all my life, so thoughts come to my head which I can write about, yet I can never place them as words out of my lips. My thoughts are what if I say something wrong? What if I upset someone? Strange thing is I never felt like that with Anadhi and Erasmus, or their son Jacobus.

Even then, I never asked why mother and son seemed the same age. I knew I would find out as I read the Kasteel Vrederic diaries. Until then, I would wait.

Uncle James laughed as he said, "You think a lot, but you don't say anything. Is it because you are shy, or because you were prevented from saying anything?"

I watched them and felt like I couldn't get anything out of my mouth yet I wanted to say and ask so much. It was then I saw him standing near the porch. My dream man was in a man's form, but it was just his ghostly apparition.

He watched us and asked Uncle James, "They are almost here. I am worried they will hurt Ahana and Hana. They won't stop at anything. You all need to go away and run from here. Please James, don't be stubborn as I can only do so much."

I watched Uncle James watch Aunt Agatha. They said something to one another only through their eyes.

Aunt Agatha said, "Frederic van der Bijl, did you know the Frederick Philipse I, the Lord of the Philipse Manor in Bronx? He had built the famous haunted Old Dutch Church of Sleepy Hollow. In Dutch, it's called Oude Nederlandse Kerk van Sleepy Hollow. It's supposedly one of the most haunted places in the United States, where I know a lot of Dutch soldiers were buried. I know you were buried there yet how is it you can travel here to this house so easily?"

I watched my dream man laugh and say, "No, I never met him as I was in the Netherlands and had just saw Jacobus van Vrederic the famous diarist was shot. My wife who had tried to heal him too was murdered. I brought my wife's ashes with me when I came here with the Dutch army. I never made it to land as I passed away on the water. I was cremated like my wife. Our ashes were scattered everywhere, some over there on the famous gravesite and some were scattered here and there, mostly in the Long Island Sound. I believe that's why I can travel around all the places my ashes were scattered. The ocean has both of our ashes. That's why we could be reborn from anywhere in the world, I presume."

Aunt Agatha watched us for a while and she then said, "I believe that's what Anadhi had told me when we were in India. If the ashes are scattered all around, you could be reborn from those places. One never knows I guess. I know there are people who have chosen to have their ashes scattered where they want to be reborn from."

Suddenly there was no sound as no one talked for a while. Scattered ashes made me wonder that's probably how I ended up in the Indian subcontinent. I just had no idea about life and death. I wonder why this subject never gave me the chills. Maybe because I always knew my twin flame and I were separated by a glass wall that's called death.

Frederic watched me and he continued, "My cousins had left some of my ashes in a jar when they lived in this house. One stormy night, the jar broke and the ashes scattered all over, getting mixed with my wife's ashes. I am assuming near here or in this house. This house actually once upon a time had belonged to my family members."

He then laughed so loudly, I worried if every one of our neighbors would hear him and find out we have a ghost friend. I questioned myself why Aunt Agatha and Uncle James couldn't see him the other day but saw him today.

Frederic told me directly, "It's because I show myself only to those of you whom I choose to show myself to. It's hard at times and at times, I can choose. I warn all of you to be careful as a lady will arrive who will say she is with social welfare. Yet she is the leader of all girls being trafficked for sex oversees. She will be very convincing but she will only try to kidnap Hana and the unborn child. I know you are thinking why she could not take any other child. Yet I know you don't want her to kidnap any child from their parents. She is the wife of the monster and is the individual who actually created this group. She married him and she has numerous boyfriends to whom she supplies girls. They are her income. Her boyfriends protect her as she protects their names from ever being publicly circulated. No one knows her real name because she goes by the name 'The Lady,' not even 'Mrs. Hunter.'"

I watched the cloudy skies get darker as the moon was missing behind the dark clouds. I knew even Mother Nature was warning us there in front of us laid danger. We couldn't ask anyone for help as even within the high-class society live the predators who kidnap children as their prey. They buy children from poor countries as sex-trafficking victims, and they bring them here as young child brides.

During my life as an imprisoned child bride, I had seen so many children from Niger brought over as child brides. They never saw any life for they became brides and then sex workers if unlucky. If lucky, they became wives who lost their childhood and all self-worth as they fell captive.

An Indian woman who was living as a housewife had once broken down in my house thinking my ex-husband was a kind soul. She told him she was a child bride. She was kept in her house as a homemaker. She never finished her education and had never been employed in her life. She had nothing for her identity except Mrs. So and So.

I had watched my animal ex-husband take advantage of her and then this innocent woman had lost her husband who was actually a good person as she became prey to my ex-husband. I don't know what happened to her as none of us saw her ever again.

Everyone on the veranda watched me as I was crying. I saw Frederic watch me as he wanted to come close and hug me. As he came closer, however, he became invisible.

He then stood far away from me as he said, "Take all precautions against her and all her friends who will try to hunt you down. Don't ever let her know you are scared of her. Remember at times, it's a warrioress who goes down fighting for truth and just. You should always know your effort has already saved so many lives. So, you have already won this battle."

I watched my foggy twin flame who looked more like a ghost and I told all, "No more will I let anyone hunt me down. I am tired of being the prey, for now I will hunt all of them down as I become the hunter. They all forgot within a woman lays a mother yet within a mother lays a snake who will not stop at biting and removing her predators to save her children at any cost. If the legal system fails, then this mother will not fail at protecting her children at any cost, even if that means this life for me must come to an end sooner than any woman dreams or wishes for."

I cried as I took Hana in my arms and kissed her head. I prayed out loud, "My Lord, protect my children, the born one and the unborn one. I was not given a dream lover or a twin flame who could protect me or love me like all women dream of being loved. At least my Lord, don't take away my children whom I have given birth and wait to give birth to as they have come to me through rape and abuse and pain. I have within my arms the small life I have fallen in love with and love with all my being. Give me enough strength to at least raise them safely or give them to someone who can raise them safely."

Aunt Agatha came over to me and said, "Let's pray the *Holy Rosary*. We will say the *Lord's Prayer*. Then, we will say *Hail Mary*, *Glory Be*, and then *Act of Contrition*.

You can say any prayer you want like my Anadhi recites *Om Namah Shivaya*. Recite any prayer your heart desires and says will protect you and your child. I was a Catholic nun all my life yet I renounced it as I knew I was meant to be with James in this lifetime and all others."

She watched us and then went to her husband and kissed him as she continued, "Actually, Jacobus my baby boy told me to ask myself and my Lord what my heart desires. If I wish to continue as a nun, then that's my future. Yet if I let James come into my life and believed James was meant to be my husband, then the Lord would understand. My faith is still very strong, but I love my Lord even more as I am happily married with my husband because that's what my Lord wanted me to have. I want you to pray and ask the Lord to guide you and be with you eternally. I also pray may you and your children have what is best for all of you."

We all saw in front of us there was a lightning bolt striking the Sands Point Lighthouse. It was invisible as then again the lightning was all over the ravishing waters where I saw an angry ghost standing and rising from the ocean.

He walked toward us as he said loudly, "You my Lord have given me nothing as you took away my beloved from me. Now give me something and let me guide my beloved and her children. Now they need help from the beyond. Maybe I can guide them like this lighthouse that had once upon a time guided so many. As this lighthouse is no longer working, may I be the guiding lighthouse."

THE GUIDING LIGHTHOUSE

Shining in the dark,

Glowing for others,

Always waiting

To see

If anyone is in

Danger,

You shine

Like the lighthouse.

Your glowing

Light helps all others,

But they don't see you.

They are guided

By you,

Yet you

Are not seen

Or heard by anyone.

I am waiting for you,

As I see how

You guide me

Without expecting

Anything

In return.

You are just standing
There ever so
Patiently and lovingly.
You don't fear them
Yet did you know
They fear you,
The one they can't see?
Yet they don't fear the
Dangers they
Can see.
I watch you and
Can differentiate
The difference
As I too
Was hunted by them.
While they think
You haunt them,
I will let all
Know you are
My beloved,
My love,
And my life.
In death,
Or in life,

I know
You are forever
For me,
THE GUIDING LIGHTHOUSE.

CHAPTER FIVE:

The Lady

"Evil is born every now and then amongst we the humans, as we the humans lose humanity and choose to practice evil."

The night seemed clear and quiet. I wanted to come back to our small cottage but I didn't want to be a burden on Uncle James and Aunt Agatha. Yet they would not have it any other way. I tried to help with dinner and felt like I was having early contractions so I had decided to sit it out. I told Aunt Agatha as she checked me and called the doctor. We waited for the doctor to call back as there were sounds outside in the yard.

I was worried for my two hosts and wondered if I had placed their lives in danger. The police had dropped off a news report from across the nation. The report was not good as it read girls young as twelve years of age are being brought into the country as wives of elderly men. Then these girls were being sold as victims of sex trafficking and some were even being held prisoners like myself and were used as domestic workers during the day and sex workers during the night.

Mr. Hunter's homes across the United States had been raided by the police. The police rescued four hundred sex workers and ten child brides. Mr. Hunter's group had actually moved all over the world and was exposed through my one report. So now, we were afraid. All over the world, they were afraid of being caught and wanted my children and me to be back in their captivity or be dead.

Suddenly we heard the crunches of leaves as if someone was walking over them. It was then I saw the front door open in front of us. There in front of us stood a woman who was dressed in all black. Her hair was long and blonde. Her blue eyes were shining in the dark. A very tall and beautiful woman, at least from the outside. She saw me and laughed like a monstress. Her laugh made me revalue my thoughts of how beautiful she was. Beauty is in the eyes of the beholders, and I revalued her as ugly as Hell.

The ugly woman said, "Hello sweetheart, it's nice to finally see you. I am the person you need to thank for rescuing you from your birth parents. I also paid to raise you until you blossomed into a flower. Now I will take your child as my reward. I will wait to have my people deliver your child and take her with me. I have enough time and I believe my doctors gave you medication in the hospital to get you to deliver early. So, I can take the baby from your womb. If needed, I will cut you open myself and take the child as the child was actually sired by my husband. So, it belongs to me. Both children do actually."

Uncle James watched her as he laughed and sat down next to her on the sofa.

He glanced at Aunt Agatha and said, "Well if born now, the baby won't survive, so you actually will lose and then the money you gambled will be gone."

The woman stood up and started to laugh like a crazy woman as she called people to enter the house. I saw there were people dressed in white who came into the house. They had masks on and had their hair covered. I could not even tell if they were men or woman as their cloaks were like medical crisis gowns.

I saw Aunt Agatha kept looking at the window as I was standing next to it. I had my child in my arms when suddenly I felt the ground next to me move and I dropped into a box under the family room. Then, I saw next to me were sitting Uncle James and Aunt Agatha. I held on to my womb as I could feel the excruciating pain hit me. I only prayed my child be allowed to see this world and not be taken away before birth for she has the right to see this painful or joyful world through her eyes.

Uncle James and Aunt Agatha told me not to talk as we walked slowly underground. I knew this was the Kasteel Vrederic family's home so they must have thought of these before they left. It was so dark I could barely see anything. Yet there in front of us Frederic was standing in his mystical form. He glowed like light and showed us the way out of the house.

We walked for a while when we finally reached another tunnel which led us to a boat parked in the Long Island Sound. We saw on the boat were two policemen who told us to get on quietly. We all walked into the boat as I watched Frederic float onto it. I imagined the policemen did not see Frederic, or else they too would have fainted.

As we sat down, I realized I was bleeding and my pain was unbearable. I held my breath under my hands as I knew very well how to suffocate my pain and the sounds from ever leaving my mouth. Yet my tears poured and I realized I still had not learned the art of controlling my tears. If only I could pour them back inside the way they poured themselves out.

I don't remember what happened next as everything was very dark and I saw the whole world had spun in front of me. I woke up in a cabin different from the one I was in before. Then I remembered I was on a boat, but this boat was not moving.

Aunt Agatha said, "Hey beautiful, how are you feeling now? I hope you are not in pain anymore. We have delivered the baby girl, and before you scream or say anything, she is well and recovering very well under good care."

She walked over and poured a cup of tea for me as she came and gave me the warm cup and said, "Jacobus had his good buddy deliver the child. He also gave his house and his car to us and has invited us to stay here until we can safely return home. The trap doors and the tunnel were built into the homes if we ever needed to escape. These homes were built centuries ago and were rebuilt by Erasmus with bunkers. This home actually belongs to Erasmus too, but is rented out by Dr. David van Peters."

I saw Uncle James walk in with a man whom I had never seen in my life. He saw me and said, "Welcome back. I am David van Peters. I went to school with Jacobus. I know I look old and for some reason my buddy still looks so young but I can guarantee, you can trust me."

He then checked my pulse and the vitals while speaking with Aunt Agatha and Uncle James. All this time, I kept searching for my two children. I was scared to ask anything in fear there was bad news and they were avoiding to tell me. I feared if the words left my mouth, then they would become true. So, I thought of only good thoughts.

I wondered had it been two whole months already since I moved in with Uncle James and Aunt Agatha? So my timing must have been all weird or my daughter was born earlier than she should have been.

Dr. David said, "Your daughter was born premature, so we had to send her to the hospital. Hana too was injured and was sent to the hospital. You were kept here so no one could link you to them and it was safer for them according to the police."

I jumped up and felt dizzy as I screamed and told them, "I knew it! My children have been kidnapped by him! You are all trying to cover up. I have not lived to see my children are gone. I lived this life because I believed even though I don't have a twin flame, I have my children as the love of my life. I survived every day as I felt my children's heartbeats. I don't want this life or my heart to beat if my children are no more. It's not fair that the Lord would take away my heartbeats from me as I can't survive without them."

I screamed and cried as I watched Aunt Agatha walk up to me and say, "Your children are alive and doing well in the hospital, where they should be. Now stop screaming and drink the tea as we will go and visit them. The police said they will bring the children to us somehow."

I stood on the balcony after this event as I watched the amazing garden of the cabin we were in. The kind doctor and his wife Mandy were entertaining us like family. Mandy van Peters introduced herself to us soon as Aunt Agatha and Uncle James gave her a strange look. I didn't say anything as I missed my girls. I felt so lonely without Hana and her sister in my womb. Also, my ghost sailor was missing. I didn't see him or my girls. It was like living but not being able to breathe. I wished I could call someone for help.

Time passed without moving at all. Days went by as I forgot to count days or weeks. Then one morning as I stood outside in the sun, I watched a car stop by our house. Two policemen were walking out of the car. They went to the back of their car and had my daughter Hana with them as one had in his arms a car seat.

Without any announcement, I ran toward the policemen as I watched Hana run toward me. I hugged my beloved child like I had not seen her in a thousand years. It was then Uncle James brought inside the car seat with my little princess. I took her in my arms and felt the heartbeats that were beating inside of my womb beat in my arms.

Then Mandy our hostess said, "She too has a heart murmur like her sister. I am a pediatric cardiologist and I do these surgeries regularly. I wanted to keep her in the hospital longer and do the surgery. Yet for some reason, Jacobus has forbidden anyone from doing any surgery until he comes.

It's as if Jacobus doesn't trust me. He and I don't get along much. He did say he will be returning in a few weeks. If it's an urgent situation, he has someone ready who could do it, somewhere I'm not sure about the location."

All I heard was Jacobus does not trust her and Jacobus is coming soon. I knew everything would be all right. I then saw with my daughters was Frederic who walked back with them. I realized he never left me as he stayed with my heartbeats all the time. He watched me and winked his eye. I should have known he would never leave the children alone with anyone, especially if Jacobus doesn't trust her.

We all gathered outside in the sunny weather walking back to the cabin when we saw the cabin of David and Mandy blow up with a big bang in front of our eyes. The ambulances and the police vans covered the grounds of the hosts.

They watched their home burn down to ashes as I told all of them, "It's all my fault. I should have known wherever I go, I take bad luck with me. I shouldn't have involved any one of you in my life. Maybe if I was gone, my children would be left alone and finally have peace. I wouldn't go anywhere until I have all of these people under the ground first. They had tried to murder my children twice now and I will hunt them down. Dear Mr. Hunter, I will become the hunter now as I take you down as my prey."

David came and hugged me as he smiled and watched me talk for so long for the first time in my life.

Mandy held me and said, "I am a doctor and my oath is to save lives at any cost, not take them. If that means we will not have a house for a while, so let it be. Material goods can be replaced my dear, but life cannot. I would save these two miraculous wonders at any cost, in any moment without thinking twice. Also, I want you to ponder on a thought. How would it have been if we were all inside of the house when the blast had taken place? We are all blessed as for the children, we all came outside. Also maybe I should just take the girls away from you now and that would save both of your daughters."

I saw David watch his wife and said, "Mandy, this home belongs to Erasmus, so it's Jacobus's home. We are only their guests. I will never separate a mother from her children, even if that means I have to give up my life."

Mandy watched her husband and her looks were very weird as she said, "You do as you want with your life. Don't bargain mine."

The police then told us it was safe for us to return to our home in Sands Point as the police were providing twenty-four-hour perimeter protection.

The two policemen who brought my daughters back were standing with us. There was a man who was in his sixties and one who was in his thirties. The younger gentleman was African American and the older gentleman was of Indian origin.

The older gentleman said, "Erasmus has called and informed us they will be back very soon. They said they have finished their private mission in Egypt and are on their way back home to the Netherlands. They will come here in a week's time. Until then, to go back home to Sands Point. Police protection is there and it's safer over there. He said he will rebuild David's house as soon as he returns and if David wants to still stay here to let him know."

The police officer walked over to his car and as he came back, there was a van with a lot of police and a lot of people in it.

He came back and then said, "Also, I want you to meet someone as we caught her and her group of people from the Sands Point house. She was here trying to set this house on fire. We had known about the blast and that's why we had all of you out of the home at a safe distance. David and

113

Mandy knew about it and actually had agreed to it as they are planning to renovate the house anyway. I would want you to see this woman and let me know if you recognize her. She said she knows Mandy."

I walked over to the van as I left my girls in the care of David. Uncle James and Aunt Agatha walked with me. In front of us in shackles was the evil woman who had tried to take my children away from me. I wondered where Mandy went because she was nowhere to be seen.

The evil woman who called herself The Lady was there and she said, "Ahh, so you survived this time, yet do know you won't next time. You alone have ruined what my husband Mr. Hunter and I had started. If he stupidly had not impregnated you or fallen for your innocence, we would have been far away somewhere in the Caribbean living a good and well-off life. You ruined our whole game. Our whole business worldwide has been exposed all because of you. Believe in my words, you won't live to enjoy your freedom very much. Also, I hate you because I don't understand why Mr. Hunter refused to give you away like he did with all of his game girls. He never impregnated anyone. Also remember, the police can't keep me away from you. They could do nothing but run away with you on a boat."

The police took her aside as they held her and pushed her inside of the van where I saw so many people were in shackles. I saw a woman there who was my nurse the last time I was in the hospital. I saw her and I told the police about her as I whispered to them.

They told us further away from the van that they knew about it. There was a man who had brought our groceries at the Sands Point house who too was in there. I was shocked to see how big of a group this was. I worried if there were more people in their group we knew and trusted.

As the prisoners left and we were brought back home, the elderly policeman told us, "This is a huge group. They won't come back here and if they do, we have people and surveillance all around, so they won't get away. My only fear is Mr. Hunter who is still on the run and hasn't been caught. I hope he left the country because if not, then we worry where he might be. The Federal Bureau of Investigation is at it now, so I know you will be safe from here on."

As everyone left I received a letter from someone and had Aunt Agatha read it out to all of us.

The letter said:

Dear Ahana,

I will have you murdered even if that's the last thing I do with my living breath. You see, I am called The Lady. That's what my people call me. Some say I was born without a heart and some say I am an evil snake in human form. Either way, I have ruined the lives of all girls or women who have come in front of me or I just want to erase. I see women as my threat as my husband was never attracted to me. He never touched me or had wanted to have children with me. He said he simply wasn't interested.

He didn't realize what powers I had, so I raised children with my own hands to have them sold off in the world bazaar as sex slaves. I make them brides as I buy them from their poor greedy families. Yes, big humanitarian organizations can't identify or quantify my victims as these victims have no voices. My workers are getting away with human trafficking.

Your global reports will never include my victims. You see I am infamously hidden as people like me are not even known to all the famous humanitarian organizations. They can never catch people like me and never tally up the victims.

You know it's so easy to convert innocence to evil but it's hard to convince evil to become good. Don't you see even Satan is more powerful than an angel? I am evil and I can't be stopped as I keep on growing throughout the world. Don't worry for me being in prison. No one can stop evil from growing, so how can anyone keep me in prison? I will escape, sweetheart, and I will see you again in my own time. Also, beware and look around you always as my people are always watching over you. I really can see you even from behind.

Until then, you can call me Mrs. Evil, or as all of my men call me, The Lady.

Signed,

The Lady

I felt my whole mind, body, and soul freeze from the inside. Yet I knew one thing that was different between the evil lady and myself. I wasn't afraid to face any evil. It was so obvious she was scared to death of being caught. She also lived to be rich and famous. She wanted to have a home on a Caribbean island and vacation forever. I wanted to be with my beloved ghost twin flame as his bride even if that meant I be his ghost bride or he be my human groom. Whenever and wherever we could be together, I would live or die happily ever after.

So, I will declare war with all of you on Earth who have robbed all girls of their childhood and who have taken away their dreams. You have taken away their teenage years, and their years of falling love and becoming someone's beloved for ever after. You have made these young girls into a one night's bride, not a bride for ever after.

So, I take a vow on this night, I will with my life or in death take away from this Earth all who take away innocence from the hearts of young girls and make them into child brides or use them as sex slaves. Tomorrow, I shall come after all of you one by one yet today, I have sent one woman to prison, she who calls herself, "The Lady."

THE LADY

From the courteous
Society
And the well-recognized
Lifestyles
You were born.
You walk amongst the
Well-off,
Well-known
Leaders,
The respectable
And recognized
Groups.
Yet I wonder,
Why you hunt
Down innocent
Underage
Children,
Those who can't speak
For themselves,
Those who can't
Fend for themselves.
You feel powerful

Knowing

You are the

Great

And the feared

One around the

Small and fearful

Ones who are your

Prisoners.

I ask you the superior

One,

Why not show

Your true color

Amongst your leaders,

Your courteous society?

Do share how you

Keep children

As child brides,

How you sell them as sex workers,

As you are recognized

And respected amongst

Your civilized

Society.

Be honest.

Be truthful.

Allow them

To see how

You have become

The rich and famous

As you have sold off

The souls of

The young

And the helpless

Children,

Whose

Blood and tears

Have today made you

In your society

THE LADY.

CHAPTER SIX:

Threatening Storm

"Storms brewing on Earth or under the sea could be witnessed by all passing individuals, yet the wild storm brewing inside a soul could not be seen or felt by anyone other than oneself."

The storm brewing outside made my heart think of him. I held my newborn daughter in my arms as I watched the rough ocean. I didn't know why I kept thinking about him and what he was doing in the storm. How do people who pass away or are ghosts live life? Do they have a home or do they wander around everywhere like floating bubbles? I would definitely feel dizzy floating as I am afraid of heights.

I wondered where I could find these answers. Somehow I felt like I needed to find out how he was. I saw a woman come inside our home. She then watched me for a while and sat on the sofa next to the windows.

She told me clearly, "Please make some tea for me. I feel like I have not had any for so long. I must be off quickly as Kees waits for me. Jacobus has been so busy for me that I actually feel guilty you are left alone and are facing all of this evil by yourself."

I jumped up in fear as I knew she was a ghost and I had never seen her in my life. She looked so beautiful and young but also looked tired and worried for some reason. I ignored her and thought this house was so old, there were probably walking and talking ghosts going around, living their own lives. I should mind my own business and let them be in peace. I thought this was all in my head and I ignored her.

She spoke again and this time said, "Dear child, are you always quiet or just plain rude? I understand my boy Jacobus has been a little busy with me and Kees, yet I wanted to see if I could somehow spiritually help you."

Then she got up and looked around the house as she loudly asked, "James, Agatha, are you two here?"

I watched Aunt Agatha and Uncle James come from the other room with little Hana. They saw this stranger and as if like magic were so happy they jumped and went and hugged her. Yes, in front of my face with my own eyes, I witnessed living humans hug a ghost.

They all watched me and Aunt Agatha said, "This is Aunt Marinda, the guiding spirit of Kasteel Vrederic. She is not a ghost but a time traveler. Jacobus is like her own son as he is very close with her as she is with him. I know you will catch all of this as you read the diaries of Kasteel Vrederic but know this. At this time, Jacobus and his entire family members are on a journey trying to rescue the woman in the mirror who is called Marinda."

I saw Aunt Marinda walk around and say, "The message is simple. Don't look for him but know he is where you are. Twin flames will unite in one life or another. Love is eternal and the blessing of love is knowing eternally he is yours as you are his. Actually in love, it matters not if you are together or separated physically, as you are eternally united spiritually. Just believe in eternal love and the rest will fall into place."

I watched Aunt Agatha and Aunt Marinda as I asked, "Is he cold or wet in the rain? Does he get hungry? Is he scared?"

The women in the room and Uncle James all watched me and said nothing as they froze like my question somehow unraveled them. I saw standing in the corner was Frederic himself.

He saw me and said, "No my dear, I don't get scared or wet or cold. I am free to be wherever I want to be. I could have been gone and reborn, yet I chose to wait for you. I will wait a hundred years more for you if I must. What I won't do is leave you alone. Please know by choice, I wait for you as I want to be with you as long as I must, so that we can awaken and rise together from the ashes all over again. This is not so bad. I get to see you and know you are safe. This is my eternal love for you, and I don't mind there is a glass fog in between us. I am blessed across the glass fog, you are there."

Aunt Marinda watched me and she came close to me as she touched my hands. I wondered how she was so much like living humans on Earth. No one actually would say she was a ghost. She could pass on like any other human. As she stayed longer, she was becoming more like a human.

Aunt Marinda said, "I am a time traveler sweetheart. I came here as Jacobus is worried about you. He told me to give you a message and let you know they have not abandoned you. They were on a rescue mission trying to unite me with my Kees, but they will be here soon. All know me as Aunt Marinda yet soon the world will know me as the woman in the mirror."

Aunt Marinda looked so young and beautiful yet how was she Jacobus's aunt? I thought I wouldn't think about it anymore as the paranormal family members of Kasteel Vrederic are just that, paranormal humans with great hearts. I knew I fell in love with this family from the bottom of my soul the day I met Anadhi.

Aunt Marinda then said, "Also my dear, you must be brave and fight to be with your beloved. Remember your children will be safe. They will not be left alone or be in danger as long as any one of the Kasteel Vrederic family members still breathes. Now, get ready for a big war as you must stand up for yourself and all the girls who the world calls child brides and are victims of sex trafficking."

Like a mist, she came and like a mist, she was gone. I felt like maybe I was dreaming. I felt so honored I just met Aunt Marinda, the great admired family member of Kasteel Vrederic. Yet I wondered what the warning was about. What war do I have to face? I thought the police had already captured The Lady.

Uncle James then said, "I felt like there were some people in the backyard, the side where land meets the water. I know we have security all around the house but somehow I have a weird feeling. Maybe tonight, we can all stick together in the family room. Let's bring both kids here and have the trap doors underneath ready for us to enter safely this time, so no one breaks their bones or gets hurt."

I felt so guilty for my two elderly family members. They were protecting me from a group of people even all the police, the FBI, and the world international crime fighting agencies were having a hard time identifying or getting rid of.

The doorbell rang as we saw David and Mandy were at the front door. Uncle James let them in as he waved his hands to the security guards guarding the front gate.

Mandy said, "I was so scared. I heard some screams or sounds of people fighting. I asked the security to bring us here to your home Agatha. We are so blessed Jacobus has allowed us to stay at the other guest cabin in your land. Yet somehow I felt maybe it's safer to be here than all by ourselves. Our phone systems are down and we were lucky the guard was patrolling at the moment we heard the sounds. We asked him if everything was okay and he said, as to his knowledge, yes, everything looks perfect."

I looked outside and thought I saw a shadow move in the backyard. Maybe it was the guards, so I wouldn't say anything to anyone or scare anyone for nothing. I got busy as I made lentil soup and rice for dinner. I had made some vegetarian curry on the side. It was not much but what I could cook. I didn't want Aunt Agatha worrying about dinner.

As it was getting late, I served dinner and we all sat down to eat. The strangest thing was no one really talked but ate their dinner as if it was our last supper. I wondered what I could do to get rid of all of this trouble. It was then my ghost sailor showed up in front of us all. I watched Mandy faint at his sight as she said, "How weirder could this night be? I can't even enjoy my dinner without being scared of gangsters coming and hunting us down. Now, we are being hunted down by a ghost."

As she fainted on top of her husband, we took her to the sofa and awakened her. Frederic came and just watched her. His face was not normal like he was trying to read her mind.

He said, "I am not evil as I have traveled time to help Jacobus and Ahana. I knew them from the seventeenth century. For all of you, it's hard to believe as you are doctors, but for Jacobus it was not hard as he lived through it. Also, how is it the evil people are scared of good ghosts and not of themselves?"

David got on his feet very quickly as he said, "Anyone Jacobus trusts, I trust too. So, let's gather up and have a plan as to what we must do ourselves to survive through the night or the days we have until these goons are all caught or we are all in a safe zone."

It was then we all saw in the front window some faces. They were looking inside. There was a face I felt like I knew but couldn't recognize as it was too dark. We all screamed and I got up first and took my two daughters in my arms. I watched my ghost sailor had in his hands taken the two from me and held on to them.

He said, "For you my beloved, I am able to hold them and I will carry both. You need to make sure you take all the others to safety. The fainted woman can remain yet make sure you take Uncle James and Aunt Agatha, as elderly people will need your guidance."

Uncle James came near us and gave both of us a stare like we had never seen. He said, "I will finish my dinner first. Then, we will all go to safety. By the way, young ghost sailor, who are you calling old? I assumed in this room, you are the only one who is centuries old. Also, it seems like Mandy is not very much liked by our ghost sailor."

I saw David mumbled as he whispered, "Strange but I can't disagree with the ghost sailor."

Frederic laughed so hard that the ground started to shake as my three-year-old daughter too laughed with him. He gave David a ghostly pat and kept on laughing.

My baby girl Hana was holding Frederic's hand as she said, "Hi friend! You're back! I missed you!"

My daughter was not aware of the situation around us and I wanted to keep it that way for I didn't want a child to ever grow up in fear or around fear.

We all finished our dinner when I saw my ghost sailor was worried and wanted us to rush. Yet we all respected Uncle James and gave our grace to the Lord first and enjoyed our meal. Then, I heard voices as they were getting louder.

One of the voices was of a woman who said, "Let's not risk anything but shoot all of them. Then, there are no worries of her or any one of them ever recognizing us. I know the doctors saw us at the hospital. Also, the elderly couple would know we were here as would their delivery people and the guys who fixed the cable lines. Our child bride had seen us visit her friends as we had forced ourselves on so many of her friends. Try to take the children alive so we can sell them for a huge amount, as they are very young. Also, maybe keep the doctor woman alive. We will need her later."

I felt like vomiting on them as I watched my daughters in the arms of Frederic.

He said, "Remember, at any cost do not separate me from the children. For I can protect them even if I can't protect all of you. So, the deal is you all will try to save yourselves and I will save these two innocent babies of my beloved."

The storm outside grew wild as the storms inside of our souls became even wilder. I prayed to my Lord for guidance as I asked him not to punish my babies or me for I hadn't done anything wrong throughout my entire life, not even to the monster I lived with.

I watched Uncle James open the trap door with a cane as I knew his feet were hurting from all of these activities.

Aunt Agatha held on to him as she said, "My beloved, whatever lays ahead of us, we will be together in life or in death. Promise me you will not risk your life without taking me along with you for better or for worse."

Uncle James then said, "Sweetheart, I won't leave you alone as I am risking both of our lives together for better or for worse. I haven't broken our given vows for anything."

I watched them walk slowly through a tunnel as we entered through the trap door. We left the trap door closed from inside so no one would know we were there. I wondered how long we would walk until we found the opening or we were somewhere safe.

It was then Mandy asked, "Could someone tell me how long we will walk for until we are in a safe and secure place?"

I saw Aunt Agatha place her hand upon Mandy's mouth. The gesture was enough though to freak her out. I wondered why Mandy talked so loudly if she knew we were in danger and sounds would travel outside. She knew everyone was asked not to talk.

I was thinking as I watched my ghost sailor Frederic whisper in my ears, "I told you not to trust anyone as we have amongst us a traitor. The same person who has been giving them all of our information. As we go forward, we will take her into the interrogations room where the police are waiting for her. Her husband has been suspecting her for a long time as she refused to have children and has been acting very suspiciously for a while."

I wondered what was going on as I thought they were both friends of Jacobus. Or was he a friend of Jacobus and she was his wife, not a friend of Jacobus? I didn't know who to trust and who not to trust anymore. As we were in their house, we were attacked and their home was burned down to ashes. How was it possible? Then again here tonight, how did someone know where we were and how did they enter through the back? That means someone had left a boat out for them to enter through the water.

It was then we entered a room that was lit with candles and had people in it. As we entered the room, Mandy started to scream and asked, "Where are we? Who are they?"

Uncle James watched her and said, "You are scared of ghosts even though you knew very well we have ghosts on the property. You were at our home long ago when you asked why there were ghostly figures all around us. Did you faint or did you act to faint? We got busy to make sure you were all right, yet I wonder what you typed on your cell phone and to whom. I thought you said you had no phone and we were asked to not use our cell phones yet you used yours in my kitchen, why?"

I watched Mandy tried to take my babies from Frederic yet they all were missing as no one knew where they were.

I wanted to scream and cry but I heard in whispers, "Please trust me sweetheart."

I knew I had promised I would be brave and quiet as the police who were sitting in the room arrested Mandy. They took her through the tunnel and were gone like a mist. We all remained quiet in the tunnel as we knew David was feeling terrible.

He said, "I don't feel bad for Mandy. She got what she was asking for. If she touched any of the children or hurt any of the children she treated or helped, I would never forgive her. I believe she was bought off with money as she always wanted to live rich. Yet I can't believe she has been trying to go against us from the hospital and the beginning."

I watched David sit down on a chair in the stone bunker. He looked like he was collapsing.

He then said, "You know Jacobus had told me years ago he has some kind of funny feeling around Mandy. He never spoke freely in front of her. He was right and I will not ponder about the past but will do whatever I must to make sure this kind of women get punished. How could a woman do this to other women and children?"

I saw Frederic return with the girls as Hana said, "I was in a huge sailing boat with Baby and Rick Ricki."

I heard my baby and ran toward her as I hugged her and my little one. I wondered but how did he take them with him?

Aunt Agatha told me, "Don't question the miracles my dear child. Question the dangers of this world and the goons that hunt us down. It's so strange I was never scared of the ghostly hauntings or the miracles from beyond, yet I am so scared of the Earthly gangsters and murderers, and above all, rapists."

I knew what she meant, yet only wished I was born in a different family, maybe to her and Uncle James. I could have had a different life all together. I wondered how I would provide for my two girls and how would I bring them up on my own. I wished my ghost sailor was here as a human and could have guided me to my destiny. Here I was worried about how I would survive and how my destiny might not include my ghost sailor. I knew I wouldn't accept a life where he isn't included, as in my mind, body, and soul, I would always have him there safely.

Like a bolt of lightning, we again heard sounds of screams outside. I wondered what the security service was doing, and why were they not able to capture a single man and his goons? It was then we all remembered the woman's voice that had come from outside of our cottage when we were trying to finish dinner. We all spoke at the same time.

David said aloud first, "Everyone, I was wondering if Mandy was the insider who was helping them, then who were the outsiders she was talking to? We all heard a woman talking about us outside of the house, remember? Who was she? Who was she talking to?"

It was so shocking as the police and the security had all left with Mandy. What about the woman outside? In the confusion, we all forgot about her. I felt like there was a new storm brewing inside of my soul. I knew I could keep myself safe from the storms brewing outside in nature by staying inside. Yet how would I protect all of us from the fearful storms brewing within my soul?

I saw my ghost sailor go through a thick wall as he came back and said, "Everyone be ready for there is coming toward us, another threatening storm."

THREATENING STORM

Mother Nature

Brews

A wild storm

Out

In the sea,

On the Earth,

And in the skies.

We were all

Forewarned,

A storm

Is coming.

The signs

Are there.

The wind

Informs us.

The pouring raindrops

Sing to us.

The rough sea waters

Cry as

All warn us

A storm is coming.

Yet the storm that

Brews inside

Of the inner soul,

The one that churns,

The one that beats fast,

The one that calls

You from

Inside,

The storm that no one sees,

Or no one hears,

Or no one is forewarned

About,

How does one

Protect

Herself from this

Unknown,

Unseen,

Unheard,

Or

Unrecognizable

Storm that brews

Inside of a soul that

Is known to

The ones

Who have felt it

And know it

As they call

It the

THREATENING STORM.

CHAPTER SEVEN:

The Hunter Is Back

"Frightened and hiding at all times, looking out everywhere in fear of what if the hunter is back."

Fear gripped all of us as we knew our ghost sailor was never wrong for he saw what we could not through the thick stone walls. We heard the sounds and knew there in our cottage was a man we feared the most. I didn't ask Frederic who was there in our home. In a strange kind of way, I knew who was there, and somehow, I didn't feel like I wanted to know. It was as if by hearing his name, he would become true. Maybe if I pretended it's not true, it wouldn't be true.

I felt the Earth shake under my feet or maybe I was shaking so hard, everything felt like it was shaking beneath my feet. Then I watched my ghost sailor stand up and actually shake the Earth. He told us to not move and just sit on the ground in a crouched position.

We did as he told us and we saw he had made an earthquake happen in front of us. I laughed at the thought of how my brain worked and I actually thought I was shaking in fear. It's not that I wasn't afraid but somehow maybe I was so scared that I was losing my mind.

David and Uncle James held my children amongst them as I held on to Aunt Agatha. We saw through a gap in the bunker, Mr. Hunter, my abusive predator, was walking in Uncle James and Aunt Agatha's kitchen. Next to him was an African woman wearing a long colorful skirt and a blouse. She also had her hair wrapped up in a colorful scarf.

She was screaming at Mr. Hunter as she said loudly, "If I don't get those babies and your darling child bride in a few hours, I promise I will have this house burned down like the other house. I lost a lot of money for you as all my girls were taken out in a raid by the police. I am financially doomed and have lost my respect and name in this society. Forever I will be humiliated by all of my friends and the society. All because I invested in you! This never happened before! You had never sired a child and all the child brides were sold to the buyers. How could you keep this prostitute for so long and sire children with her?"

I saw Mr. Hunter sit down and say to her, "Lisa, I am sorry, but you are wrong. She was not a prostitute. I had married her and she was a child bride but nothing more. I was wrong to have sold her and the children but when it's money, and more younger girls are involved, I would rather have the latter. Now, I will find them and send them overseas to them and then at least we will get out of this round. The guys will be happy. They will have two new girls they can raise and use as sex slaves."

He watched the wall we were watching them through and we all moved backward hoping he hadn't seen us. It seemed like they didn't see us.

Then, Lisa asked Mr. Hunter, "Dear man, I hope seeing your child for the first time doesn't give you any fatherly feelings. I know you tried to rape your own child but you weren't successful, or was it you didn't want to? Hmm, you don't have any answers, do you?"

I was enraged with anger as I knew he was a monster and I wanted to scream and tell him that. Somehow my ghost sailor placed his hand on my mouth and prevented me from uttering anything. I was shocked at the touch as his hands were neither hot nor cold yet somehow I remembered his touch and I felt like I was in the seventeenth century.

I was crying for my husband when I was shot and I asked Rietje to take my body to my husband because he wouldn't survive without me. I remembered I had no children and worried if I could ever have children. We had so wanted to have our own children but couldn't. I cried for Frederic and called his name as I shouted and screamed for him but my breath was so slow, and the words didn't come out but just whispers.

It was then my ghost sailor moved his hand off my mouth, and I jumped back into the present time.

I held him in my arms and told him in a whisper, "Why my beloved did we not have a chance last life? I had died and in this life, you are not amongst the living but amongst the dead."

He kissed my head as he said nothing but just saw my tears and wiped them with his ghostly hands. He showed me what was happening in the other room by pointing toward the kitchen.

We all saw Mr. Hunter had a gun in his hands as he tried to see if there was really an earthquake happening. He crouched down on the floor as did his female friend Lisa. Frederic made the Earth shake even more.

It was then I saw Lisa fall to the ground and shriek in fear as she said to Mr. Hunter, "I don't want to die in your mistress's house. I will not have anything to do with this anymore as I want to get out of all of this. I will tell the police I was forced to come here by you and your gangsters. I will save my own soul. You can go and be with the dead."

I watched Mr. Hunter get up and hold her by the hair. He pulled her to the ground and said, "You will do as I tell you bitch. I have enough proof of your actions sent to all my social media websites. They will be published tomorrow if I don't manually stop them by then. So you bitch can scream or shout as much as you want but I will not go down without taking you down with me. By the way, all the other members of our hidden society too will be exposed tomorrow if I don't make it out safely. That means I must have a way out of this country with all the luxuries of life to make sure you and all your leaders and societal gurus are left unscratched by these rumors."

It was then I heard my baby girl cry and knew we would all be exposed if we didn't either run away or hide the sound somehow. David panicked and started to whimper in fear. I watched Frederic take my baby girl in his arms and rock with her as he then made sounds of a raccoon purring on the front lawn.

Lisa asked Mr. Hunter, "What was that sound? I felt like it was a baby crying. It must be your newborn child. Your child bride had the child, remember? Mandy told us she was born. So, it was her."

I saw Mr. Hunter glanced outside and said, "I just saw a raccoon run that way. Raccoons cry like babies."

The pair watched outside as I swear there were raccoons running out there. I wanted to get out and just face my predator. Maybe then, he would leave my children alone.

Uncle James whispered in my ear, "At times it is better to know your enemies and it's safer to keep them at bay. Watch and learn about their actions. Don't give any reason for them to come after us. We are in a rocky boat. While they have the upper hand, we don't. We must wait to have the upper hand and then go after them."

I knew he was right. At this time, I needed to keep my anger at bay for the sake of everyone here. I watched another earthquake hit our small kitchen. Pots and pans were flying everywhere. I watched a pan fall on top of Lisa's head as I saw my ghost sailor standing in the kitchen in front of the predators.

He placed a huge slap on Lisa's face as she got furious and slapped Mr. Hunter back. Then, I saw she had placed her gun on him and tried to shoot him.

Mr. Hunter said, "Lisa, don't try anything funny. I will leave you dead in this kitchen without mercy."

Then, I heard the police car alarm sound loud as the front doors opened and let the security see how these two were in the house. The police came and I watched them shoot Lisa down. Mr. Hunter ran toward the back and we all saw a speedboat sail far away, very quickly. The footsteps of a few people joined the speedboat as Mr. Hunter walked on it and watched our home. I could swear I heard him say, "You have not heard or seen the last of me. I will be back."

After a long time of silence, we all got out from our hiding bunker. My ghost sailor then said, "That's not the last of him. I know we will soon be repeating, the hunter is back."

THE HUNTER IS BACK

Hiding from him,

Running away

From him,

Keeping oneself

Quiet,

So, he stays away,

As you fear his touch,

You fear his

Evil glares.

You stay hidden,

Safely within

Your own home.

Yet he is not afraid.

He is not scared.

He is not ashamed

Of his actions

As he is the predator

Who only lives

To

Take

His prey

And make them

Weak,

And make them crawl under

Their bed,

Or hide in the closets,

As they know

If they ever forget

Or try to

Erase you

From their minds,

You the raider

Will keep

On knocking on the

Doors of your prey

And tell them

THE HUNTER IS BACK.

CHAPTER EIGHT:

Hunted Becomes The Huntswoman

"Weak and destitute have no friends in the world of evil and the powerful, except when the victims awaken and to protect themselves and their loved ones, they become the hunters."

James Brown, the well-respected author and dream psychic, had now armed himself against all unwanted intruders. He brought out his guns and was getting ready to fight with the intruders. Aunt Agatha watched him as did David. I stood at the doorway with my ghost sailor and wondered why Aunt Agatha was so upset.

She saw me and said, "Your Uncle James actually does not believe in guns and that's why he keeps all of them empty. We have them for safety as we live alone and at times, we worry how to we protect ourselves in a world of mistrust and dishonesty. I remember how my Anadhi, her grandmother, and I had traveled around the world all alone looking for Erasmus. It never came to our minds we might have to actually face criminals like these."

She went near the fireplace and touched a family portrait in which she was holding Anadhi. She kissed the picture and said out loud, "I love you so much my dear. At times, I feel like I have to hug you at least once to even go on."

I knew I must stand on my own feet and help the Brown family. I didn't like talking about guns or anything. The thought of my gun taking the life of another human being is something I could never live with. The bullet enters the person and he stops breathing. Never could we bring him back, even if we tried.

I observed my ghost sailor and asked him in my mind, "How did you die my beloved? I always wondered yet could never ask. I remember I had a bullet shot at my back in my last life. The small powerful thing took my breath away and I couldn't even talk or breathe as I laid there on the ground dead."

I didn't realize I had spoken out loud and Uncle James was watching me as he sat down on the kitchen chair and started to brush his hair backward with his hands. He observed me and Frederic as he picked up Hana from the floor and sat her on his lap.

He then asked, "How did you die Frederic?"

I watched my ghost sailor and waited for his answer. Frederic looked at all of us and said, "I was shot on my back. It was strange because I thought the man who shot me was actually the co-captain. I was the captain of the ship. As we were ready to dock, everyone was getting their weapons ready even though I told everyone we were in safe area and everyone could relax. We planned to stay there for a while. It was nearly dark and my co-captain was trying to get his gun unjammed. Suddenly while he was checking it, the gun accidently unjammed on me. He was scared and told everyone the truth. He took my body back to the Dutch burial ground and found in my belongings my wife's ashes. So they cremated me and I was scattered everywhere, so I could be with my wife. He did scatter some of my ashes and my wife's ashes in the ocean."

It was like listening to the end of a very tragic storyline. I thought why I had asked him for the details. I started to cry and thought why all love stories had to end with tragedy.

Frederic laughed and came near me as he said, "Sweetheart, our love story here began with tragedy. How do you see it ending? Forever we will have this wall of separation which is called life and death. Yet think how blessed we are to be together in life or death. Our love story will be retold by the living and the dead. I would rather be with you than be alive and separated from you."

I tried to hug him but only could fold my hands and hug myself. I felt cold and shivered in fear. I didn't know what I could do to make myself feel any better or worse. I laughed and thought maybe I was going crazy.

I told my ghost sailor, "Hey sailor, think of it this way. People fall in love and then get married and then have children. I had children and then fell in love with a ghost sailor. So now, my love story shall never end as it started with death and will actually continue even beyond death. As long as you wait for me, I promise to be yours all my life and will be the ghost bride after my death."

Everyone in the room was crying and then David got up and said, "Actually, I love your plan and maybe our captain can have a boat big enough, ready for more sailors to join him as we all are heading his way, sooner or later."

I laughed and felt better as I saw David wink at me and knew everything would be all right. All love stories end, yet my love story won't end as it will continue even after death.

Uncle James stood up and said, "I don't believe in guns or taking life. I actually don't even hunt as we are both pescatarians. I will, however, keep the guns ready so no one in this life takes my babies away from me. My two little darlings Hana and her baby sister whom we need to name will be protected at any cost. I will keep the guns ready for anyone who tries to come near my family members. Even though I don't believe in guns, I must take upon my hands the choice to protect and save my family, if it is needed."

I knew what he was saying as I watched the front yard and thought about how long we had been scared. We trusted the police. We trusted the security forces, and even then we were being hunted down from inside of our own home and from oversees. These monsters were hiding amongst the wealthy and privileged ones of the society.

It's so weird how these crimes were still being hidden under the rugs. The former governor of New York, Governor Cuomo, had signed into law that child brides are illegal in New York State. Yet he could not make it illegal worldwide. If only people could see these child brides are also being used as sex workers. I guess it's true that people don't see what they don't want to see, even if it's in front of them.

I wouldn't let my fear get in the way. I would have at least one goon put out of the way, even if it's the last thing I do in my life. I would not be afraid of you anymore Mr. Hunter for I have become the huntswoman. Scared and frail, sitting in a dark corner waiting for the pain to subside, I was for years. Yet now I wait with excitement for you to come in front of me for I will ask you then why you did this to me.

Aunt Agatha stood up and said, "Ahana, you should relax and maybe rest for a while. You're still bleeding and you haven't had enough to eat or drink as you need your strength to take care of these babies. I am worried who will take care of them if you get injured or ill."

Aunt Agatha's face looked frail and tired. I worried she was taking too much on herself. I got up, went close to her, and I gave her a big hug. I kissed her head and held on to her for a while.

I told her, "I wish I could have reversed time and had been born to you and Uncle James. If only I could reverse time and make it happen. Yet I am blessed to know you, and I am happy even in this situation, I have found you."

It was then we heard big thundering noises coming from outside. I thought no way would any human come banging in like that in front of the security forces. They would be outrageously stupid to do that. Yet I heard big banging sounds.

My ghost sailor was again missing as we knew he was trying to observe the situation.

He came inside and said, "There is someone out there who has placed a door of some kind and I can't see through it. That means Mandy has told them about me and they have someone powerful who is trying to stop me from helping."

We all tried to see what was going on as I saw Uncle James was trying to think about something. He watched his wife as they spoke mind to mind. I realized Uncle James must have had a dream where he saw something bad.

Aunt Agatha got up and said, "Let me have them now. I will make sure this story ends on our terms, not on the terms of the sex traffickers."

David held on to the girls and was trying to hide them under the table as we heard bullets were being fired. I wondered what I could do to change the situation. What could I do to maybe change Mr. Hunter and at least get some help from there? I remembered his face and thought how could I change the beast as he had nothing inside of him but beastly sexual desires? He sees or feels for nothing but himself.

Frederic said, "During any war, you could be the best army if you learn to be patient and wait for the opposition to come to you. Don't let yourself be seen but watch out for them. We will wait it out and let them lose their patience."

Frederic then walked to the door and saw me for a while. He picked up Aunt Agatha's cross and her bible in his hands as he walked out of the door without opening the door. Even in this situation, I started to laugh.

Aunt Agatha asked me, "What happened? Why are you laughing by yourself? You haven't lost your mind, right?"

I couldn't stop laughing. As always with me, I start laughing for no reason and have a hard time controlling myself.

I told them, "It's because I thought he was going to open the doors to go out. I worried then he would expose my girls and all of us to the beast and his goons. I guess my ghost sailor realized and did his eyebrow thing, like 'really?' It's then I realized at times I forget he is a ghost."

I got Uncle James giving me his eyes and basically asking me to be quiet and watch out for him.

Uncle James went closer to the window and said, "I will keep an eye out for him and I am ready with my gun if he needs assistance."

Everyone laughed at Uncle James as we all said at once, "He is a ghost."

It was getting late and I could not see where he went. It irritated me more that I could not go with him than where he was.

I watched David staring at the ceiling fan and felt dizzy thinking how he could stare at it like that.

I asked him, "David are you okay?"

He watched me and said, "I was trying to think what the purpose of my life was. Never had children as Mandy couldn't have any. Now I have taken a year off from work and will be trying to get back on my feet alone and maybe actually happier. I will sign up as a volunteer with Jacobus's foundations, if he will have me. That way, I could devote my life to doing something for the people of this world instead of always thinking about the same old thing, what about me? Yes, that would give me so much pleasure. Maybe I could help myself by helping others too."

When David stopped talking, I heard more bullets firing and knew we had some kind of holdout outside.

Frederic walked in and said, "I have made some progress. Now they are thinking the police are firing outside. They have some kind of a voodoo lady here who is doing some kind of crazy dance and is trying to keep the dead or evil out of here. I walked past her and asked my Lord to protect me for my beloved and her family. I realized then just because I am dead, that does not make me evil or the living good. So, I had no problem going around her. She killed the security officers out there. There were two security cars that are missing too."

He stood up and tried to check something outside as he then picked up my newborn baby and let her sniff out something.

He kissed her head and said, "She still can sniff him as he is her biological father. The older one can't because she hates him too much to sniff any good or bad. I hope he too does not sniff her out. I know he is somewhere nearby."

He then handed back my child as he blew out a huge windstorm from his mouth. We all watched him as he kept on doing it. From nowhere, there was a huge windstorm that came from nothing. The trees were all blowing so hard and the branches flew everywhere. I heard people outside screaming who were trying to take shelter.

Things were flying on top of our roof and the wind was banging against the windows. I watched my ghost sailor talk to Uncle James in his mind as Uncle James only nodded to his question.

The wind gust was getting worse. A woman outside said, "I am going inside. I will shoot your child bride and the two girls myself and end all of this. Then, we can go into hiding until everything gets calm again. I think things have gone crazy as we are all being hunted down by the FBI, the local police, and the international security forces. Our pictures are everywhere on all websites and all international airports. I have had enough."

It was then we saw the doors burst open as a huge group of women entered the house, armed with machine guns that could take out Uncle James's guns at any second. My only hope was Frederic as I saw he was standing in front of my girls as a shield. He came with the girls near me and covered all three of us.

David walked in front of Aunt Agatha and Uncle James as a shield. It was then again another windstorm came and the back door opened as I watched all the women being blown out of the house like leaves. I was shocked how all of this was happening. Yet I knew and believed in miracles.

The whole house filled up with leaves and broken branches, yet there were no signs of any women or men or nay human being as all were somewhere under the deep blue ocean.

I asked Frederic, "Are they all dead?"

He watched me again with his face in a shock mood and did the eyebrow thing again.

He laughed and said, "I am not a murderer. They will all be sent to the lighthouse under the branches. They will have bruises yet will survive. I hear the jail cells are ravenously awaiting their arrival."

I wondered if we were all out of danger yet. Or was the biggest danger still out there? Where was he and why was he so strong? It was then I heard another familiar voice.

It was Mr. Hunter's voice and he said, "Senator, I understand your reputation is in question here yet I have no control of the situation. You started the game and wanted children as sex toys. These men who were marrying these women under the falsehood of child brides are all going under. They don't want to be linked to any of these things. I can't bring any more children here as child brides. My two daughters are not available as I would ask you to take your own child, not mine Senator. I will find my girls and have them killed as I don't want to see a monster in their eyes when they see me anymore."

I didn't know what to think. I wondered if he was saying all of this to make me hear that he does have some heart in his tin man body, or he was changing, or maybe he just got caught and doesn't know what to do.

I was absolutely blank when suddenly a door opened in front of us and there in front of us was a woman who looked so familiar. She was white with brown hair. Yet her eyes told me she was of mixed race somehow.

She walked in and asked Uncle James directly, "I have had enough of this rubbish. Give me the children. I will take them with me and then all the security forces will come back. You all will be in peace as if nothing had ever happened. You fools, why did you not think how the security and the police all just disappeared like thin air when you needed them? They are all in my control. Yet I don't know who it was on our side that was killing our bribed police officers and making all of this chaos."

She looked so familiar as Uncle James said, "Senator, I don't believe this. Why would you even be involved in this kind of criminal activity."

She laughed and said, "It's my passion. I provide for men, and they provide me with money and fame. Now I am a senator. I am able to do this crime which no one else can do."

Aunt Agatha walked in front of my two girls and Frederic as Hana was sitting on her highchair and her baby sister was sitting in her car seat.

Hana started to cry and said, "Dada no hurt me. No hurt my baby."

Mr. Hunter was standing at the open door of the cottage. I saw he watched Hana and then saw my little newborn baby sitting in her car seat. She had her little pink fingers crawled in a fist near her mouth. She either laughed or burped in her sleep. Mr. Hunter walked to the girls and stood in front of them.

The woman came closer laughing like a maniac as she said, "Let's get rid of them now and we begin again when the water clears."

Mr. Hunter then said, "No, I will not shoot my own children. I tried to rape my own daughter because you installed a camera and told me if I didn't, then you would have all of them killed. I will tell you now, you can have all the girls in this world but not my children. I have been killing your goons trying to protect Ahana and the girls as I am their criminal. I committed so many crimes that I can't even count them. Yet today, I ask you leave this household and I will never link you to me or any of these crimes. I will hand myself to the authorities after I know Ahana and her girls are safe."

The woman had a gun out and said, "It's strange how I never suspected you to even grow a heart. I actually thought you were a tin man. I guess if you want anything done, you have to do it yourself. Also, Mandy lied about ghosts and spirits. There are two elderly people. She might have thought they were ghosts."

She then started to laugh like a crazy maniac as she told everyone to close their eyes. She was laughing out loud as I saw Mr. Hunter wink at me.

Frederic said, "Ahana, move away. I will take care of the babies. Just move away from here. I don't like the woman's thoughts. She is all evil."

It was then things got worse. The woman started to aim her gun toward my daughters. She was calling some people with her whistle as they came running in and stood behind her. She ordered everyone to get ready. My daughters began to cry at the sound of the whistle. It was the first time I saw Mr. Hunter look at them, as if maybe he too was worried.

She said, "Like military style, get rid of everyone and make sure Ahana and her girls don't live through this to ruin any other person's life. They have caused enough devastation as I have had enough of them."

It was then I saw a gun fire toward my two babies. My ghost sailor stood in front of them ready to take the bullets yet they went through him. My feet rushed before my mind could think as I jumped in front of my babies. Someone else beat me and stood in front of them.

Mr. Hunter said, "I helped bring these children to this world. I also caused all the pain and anguish and ruined all of your life. I ruined anyone I touched as I am a monster to all I have touched. May my death mark the end of a sex trafficker who forced a child to be a bride. May my children never see me or anyone like me ever in their life. I pray if God can listen to me, may my children not even remember me."

I watched Mr. Hunter stand up with blood gushing out of his chest as he went near the shocked woman and shot her with Uncle James's gun he picked up from the quivering hands of Uncle James. He then gave a note to Uncle James as he fell to the ground. I watched the nightmare unfold in front of my eyes which I never believed would ever happen.

Then I picked up Uncle James's gun as I saw my ghost sailor was fighting a battle no one saw he was fighting yet he was winning.

I held my gun as did Uncle James, David, and Aunt Agatha. We all picked up our weapons and walked outside.

I shouted with my lungs out and told everyone, "Come everyone and witness history today, as you will all see how the hunted becomes the huntswoman."

HUNTED BECOMES THE HUNTSWOMAN

Afraid of you,

Hiding from you,

Giving you power,

As I the hunted

Am powerless.

I would rather be safe

Than fall prey

And be sorry.

Yet at

All times,

I remain hidden

Under the blanket

In fear,

Under the bed,

Out of safety,

I hide.

Yet what happens

When you

Make I the innocent

Your victim,

Your prey,

Over and

Over again?

You hunt,

I hide.

You torture,

I tolerate.

You play

A game

Of run

And catch,

As I keep running.

You then keep on

Catching.

Yet do remember,

You have created

This game.

You have taught

Me well.

As your victim, I watched,

I monitored

Your games.

Now, I

With honor,

And just,

With truth,

And fairness,

Have awakened

As I the

HUNTED BECOME THE HUNTSWOMAN.

CHAPTER NINE:

Shattered Wings

"A beloved is born to be loved and kept safely within the protection of her beloved's arms, not so her wings could be shattered under terror."

ar began in our home as we armed ourselves against the hunters. I watched Mr. Hunter hold on to the girls as we all fought an ugly battle no one in our neighborhood even knew was going on. I watched how David, a doctor, tried to treat Mr. Hunter. He told us, however, there was nothing he could do but let time take its course. I watched Mr. Hunter pass away and he was actually smiling as his life ended.

He said, "Little Angels, I could not be there for you during life as I was your predator, yet I pray with my death you two get a loving home where you two will grow up knowing only love and happiness."

Frederic walked next to me and he said, "Maybe death agreed with him. It's not so bad if you accept it lovingly. Sometimes it's the end and sometimes it's the beginning. I wait to find out how I can unite with you through the door of death and life."

I didn't answer him as I told myself I would wait and watch the Earth and her beautiful glory until I can finally unite with my ghost sailor man.

The night ended with the runaway army of the senator. The paper Mr. Hunter gave Uncle James had the name of a detective whom Mr. Hunter was working with to protect all of us. He tried to convince his group to leave us alone and tried to work with them and be here trying to work against them. All the time, he wanted to expose the senator. Strange thing was she was not found even after all the searches the detective and his army of police officers had done.

The morning came with the sun shining across the Long Island Sound. I walked along the shore and watched the water flow. It was an amazing sight as how peaceful everything seemed at times and how it all seemed so dark and scary at times. The difference was not the nature but our own minds.

Aunt Agatha brought a fresh cup of tea for me as she said, "Everything is calm right now. The house has been cleaned and all the damages are being repaired and paid by the security company. I know as you probably have seen James is very unsettled. He knows something he won't share with me, but it is eating him up."

I hugged Aunt Agatha for a while as we drank our tea and watched the water flowing so calmly. The sun's ray on the water was magical. It was then I thought I saw something in the water. Both of us watched the water and the Sands Point Lighthouse, yet we saw behind the lighthouse so big and tall was a sailor standing. His body shined like the sun as he had his hands out toward us like a call from the beyond.

I saw him calling me and saying my name. I stood up and started to run toward him as I forgot I could not walk on top of the water. I remembered I never learned to swim as I was sent away as a child bride before I could learn or experience life. I cried and was shocked as I felt Aunt Agatha wake me up.

She said, "Sweetheart, you were dreaming. Remember we have sent Mr. Hunter's body to the police to handle it as per his request. Everything is back to normal and the security company will pay for all the damages."

I told her about my dream and told her it seemed so real. I told her, "In my dream, I was so relaxed but I knew there was something more to it. It was if you actually were sitting on the bench by the water and I was sitting there next to you. Yet I know something was off. I felt like I could walk on water as I saw Frederic rise from beneath the ocean. I too wanted to rise with him. I felt like my wings were shattered and I could not go with him as I fell. I felt like a shattered bird whose wings were broken and couldn't fly."

Uncle James walked in the room as he said, "Everyone, I made poffertjes or in America, we call them small pancakes. A Dutch breakfast to get everyone smiling again."

I walked outside with my two girls as somehow I hoped at least Hana would be unmindful to the happenings of the house. Yet she was not.

She said, "Mom, where is Dada? When Piano Papa coming? I want to go home."

I watched her and Uncle James said, "Who says adopted children are not like their parents? You have already picked up after me. You are a dream psychic. I am blessed you are just like me."

It was then they all realized I was still listening. I knew what the message was but I tried to be brave and not worry about the future. I didn't want to worry about the future. I would never marry anyone as long as I lived. How could I ever think of someone else when I knew who my twin flame is? For I will save all my love for him and only him.

I wondered why he was not here this morning. I missed him so much. If only I could be with him anywhere, anytime. My baby girl cried as I watched David take a look at her. I knew his inner doctor comes out now and then as he keeps on planning his schedules as to when he could fly oversees and be of help to the people who so much need his help.

Aunt Agatha finished her pancakes as he sat with her coffee and gave me a fresh cup of tea. She then gave her husband his coffee and sat next to him on their comfy couch.

Aunt Agatha then said, "Something that still bothers me is Mr. Hunter's whispers to James. He said she will not stop and will come back to get revenge. I believe he was talking about the senator as no one found her dead or living body anywhere."

I stood up and didn't know what to do or how I could leave and maybe not risk the Browns anymore. I had no college education and no experience in any work force. Where could I start? How would I find a job to support my two daughters and myself?

Uncle James smiled back at me and said, "Don't worry yourself too much. Mr. Hunter told me before he passed away, he left all of his homes, his savings, and his bonds in your name. He said he knew it would be enough to take care of you and the children for life. Maybe he didn't provide during his life but he did eventually do it after his death. He also said these properties and money are from his forefathers, not from his business."

I watched Uncle James and knew everything would be all right now, yet why was I so panicked? What if something goes wrong and I happen to die? What would happen to my two girls?

Aunt Agatha said, "The attorneys are coming soon to help with all of these things. Don't you worry about anything. Your kids will be just all right. The only worry is how and where do we find this woman?"

The police were again at our home as they had huge dogs with them this time. I didn't see my ghost sailor all day, so I was a little cranky. I wondered do I worry about a dead human or should I worry about the living ones? I tried not to think about him when the barking dogs scared the wit out of me.

Then, he was there as he said, "So, not scared of ghosts, or being held under the guns of the goons yet scared of dogs? That's so strange."

I saw him and felt so lonely even though he was next to me. If only I could see him even once in the form of a man, I would be happy eternally.

He then asked me, "Would you really be happy if you saw me just once? Or you would then want to see me even more?"

I was so furious he read my mind, I didn't answer him. I knew he would read my mind anyway. I wondered if I could really be with him eternally or if he could come to me and be here with me eternally.

I said nothing as I knew I hurt him by these thoughts. It must be hard for him as it was hard for me too. The dogs barked for a while as it seemed the barking became louder and louder.

I feared something wrong was going to happen. I started to cry as I held on to my two babies. What would happen to them if I actually floated over to the world with Frederic? What about my baby girls? I had a sinking feeling something was very wrong.

It was then I saw my ghost sailor come and stand in front of me. He was crying and it was strange I could feel his tears fall on my hands. I asked him are you becoming a human or am I becoming a ghost?

He just watched me and said, "Last night, I tried to save the girls. I tried to take them away with me, but I think I have been here for so long or maybe I have used so many powers allowed for a ghost to have that I could do nothing. I am blessed Mr. Hunter saved them as he left the world. Maybe it was his miracle to perform and not mine. Yet I felt so bad, I stayed away all day today."

It was then we saw the woman senator walk out from our fireplace just like she never left. She was bleeding and was laughing at the same time. I don't know if she was half dead or half alive, but she was able to see Frederic.

Aunt Agatha and David stood in front of the children who were left alone by the sofa next to the door. In between the door and the sofa and Aunt Agatha and David was the senator.

I knew the woman was capable of doing anything right now. Uncle James had put away his guns in hope the senator had left and we were not in danger anymore. I felt like the Earth under my feet just moved and I had no solid ground left beneath my feet.

My wings were so far away, I could not protect my babies with these shattered wings. I looked at Frederic for help. Any help would be all right as I needed a miracle right then.

The woman sat down on the coffee table with her feet up and asked for a cup of coffee. She asked David to heal her wound. I watched the doctor in front of me help heal the woman who had been destroying so many lives across the world.

I asked her, "How many wings did you shatter around the world? How many little girls did you ruin? Why did you not fear ruining other girls and women as you too are a woman, a girl, who should feel and know the pain of a woman? I wonder if you ever had any soul or were born without one."

Then my ghost sailor was gone. The woman screamed when she saw the medical bags David was using were thrown outside of the front door. The woman screeched like a monster and started to shoot all around the house blindly. She had a lot of guns stored in her pants pockets. I felt like she was dressed to kill all on her path. Maybe she wanted to dress like a goon before her last ritual.

I told her, "You are so scared of being exposed yet don't you know living or dead, you will and have been exposed. Since you don't fear death, you should know neither do I. I will hunt you down even after my death if that's what I must face today, yet even death won't take away the chance of having a normal life for my daughters."

I watched her fire blindly as her anger was getting bad. I watched Frederic try to make an earthquake happen again. The ground started to shake as the woman screamed like a monster.

She screamed and screeched, "I will kill you first and then I will take your girls. I won't kill them. I will shatter their wings in their childhood. I will sell them in an open bazaar where they take children as child brides and convert them to income earners as sex workers. There is no one in this world who would come now and help you all."

That's when we saw a few women come in and tied everyone with ropes. They took my babies and placed them in their car seats. I wondered if Frederic could help us somehow.

He tried to shake the lights and throw them on the woman but she did not barge or move. I didn't know why he wasn't able to do much as somehow, he seemed tired and weak.

The senator laughed as she watched Frederic directly and said, "Frederic van der Bijl, a Dutch Eighty Years' War warrior. You died strangely as I know somehow it was not normal. I have been to your gravesite and I know there is no body over there. So where were you buried? Under the ocean? Hmm, I also know some ghost hunters who can make you weak. Just wait and see what happens."

I wanted to cry for Frederic, but he told me mind-to-mind, "Don't believe her. She is a politician and bluffing is how she made her life's earnings. I am fine and won't fear her. I just don't want to hurt my little angels by shaking the Earth or anything else. I know though help will come, yet I just hope it's not too late."

The woman got up and said, "I changed my mind and I think I will have the girls killed too. So, we won't have any more trouble left over for us to face in the future. Ladies, start shooting one by one as I've had enough of this drama. Now let's finish up quickly and we can all go and have a nice dinner afterward."

I watched the woman grab my daughters as if she was going to kill them first. I screamed and somehow untied my hands. I knew Frederic had our hands untied. He slowly went and stood in front of my daughters as he threw both of them outside. My girls were flying in the wind.

I heard him pray, "My Lord, give the girls to their parents now and let them live. I will give up anything on and beyond to save the girls of my beloved for I too feel like they are mine."

It was then I saw from somewhere came a familiar looking woman and a man running and trying to catch the two girls.

The woman was crying as she ran as fast as she could and said, "Andries, catch the child! I will catch the baby!"

I watched the two catch my babies in their arms as the woman ran to the man and both of them held my two girls in their arms.

I heard my baby girl say, "Mama and Piano Papa, you come for baby and me. Let's play again."

I saw then Anadhi walked in with Erasmus and Jacobus. Anadhi went in front of the gun holding woman and slapped her face as she single-handedly took the weapon.

Anadhi said, "No one hurts my family members on Earth or beyond. Wherever you go, you will find your karma waiting for you."

I saw everyone in the room and wondered why everything seemed fuzzy. It's then like a whisper, I heard my famous doctor talking.

I realized I was somewhere else where I felt a soft bed under my body as I heard words very softly around me.

Jacobus was saying, "I need your permission to have the girls as my nieces. You don't have much time left sweetheart. Please know where you are going, my brother had also been to. The one who will adopt your girls. He told me to tell you not to be scared and to walk directly through the reincarnation door. Remember to take your twin flame with you through the door with you. He is right here waiting for you."

I was not in any pain yet wondered what had happened. I heard Jacobus talk with the others as he said, "The woman shot Ahana as she lost the girls. No one even realized, neither did Ahana as even she was busy watching her two daughters fly out in the air. I realized as I saw her eyes were dazed, looking at her daughters. Frederic was holding on to her so I am assuming she didn't feel anything as he was able to take her pain away for her. It's weird as they are twin flames. So, they must unite in life or in death. I guess the senator would have shot either the babies or Ahana. I actually think Ahana would have it no other way."

I felt the teardrops of Jacobus and told him, "I promised I would keep your lineage safe. Now Jacobus, you keep my children safe as they too are my gifts for your family and they are your lineage."

I signed the papers like I still didn't know why everyone was so worried as I felt great. I only wondered how my life had ended so soon. I am only eighteen years old and in this time period I have witnessed abuse, rape, childbirth, and I will forever be known as a child bride.

My life story tells a story of a girl who was sold for a few bucks. I tried to be a brave girl as I never cried with physical pain or emotional pain either for I was told girls are not allowed to even cry. I had no chance in life as I was born with shattered wings.

SHATTERED WINGS

Born to be sold,

In the market,

In an open bazaar

For money

To buy food

To keep the family

Going,

I was sacrificed

At the wedding altar.

I laid

Dead

Yet alive

For I realized

This was not

My playhouse

Where my dolls would

Be married,

But

I, a child, would

Give birth

To real

Babies,

As I,

A child,

Had to grow up

And make sure

My real dolls,

My babies,

Are never

Sold

Or have their wings broken

As I could

Never fly,

Nor could I

Protect myself,

Yet I will

Protect my babies

At any cost,

Even from the beyond,

As today

After a

Short-lived life,

I must fly away

As

I lay powerless.

All my dreams are

Shattered.

All my future

Plans,

My nightly dreams, and

My daydreams,

Washed

Away in

The

First

Waves

Of the rough sea.

My dream house

And my

Dream life

Wash away

Like

A sandcastle,

Which never

Had

A chance,

As

With the

First waves

Of the rough sea,

My dream castle was

Crushed

Like it was never,

Ever a dream

Castle.

Yet I lay happy

As I know

I have left my

Babies

Protected

In a family,

Where they will have

Their own wings

And will never be

Like their mother,

Who was born

Without any chance in

Life

Of having any dreams

Becoming

A reality

As I

Was born

Broken.

I was born

Injured,

For I the innocent dove

Was born

With

SHATTERED WINGS.

CHAPTER TEN:

Rising From The Ashes

"Forever together in life or death, twin flames rise again and again from the ashes only to unite forever again."

T he journey through the tunnel was like a dream as I walked with my beloved. We saw there was a door which had a sign that said, "THE DOOR OF REINCARNATION." We entered and then we saw on the door, there was a message that said, "Until birth, you can wait here in the tunnel of light, or as you were granted freedom, you can go and visit your family members and choose to rise together from the ashes."

I saw like my dreams, we both were rising from the sea. This was so familiar as I knew this was where I had been originally. I knew this was Naarden, the Netherlands. We were both back home in the Netherlands.

Frederic said, "Sweetheart, are you positive you want to see this because they won't be able to see us. We will only have a short period of time and then we both will be reborn to reunite as twin flames."

I watched the castle which was once upon a time my home. I walked into the castle where I saw my daughter Hana walking with Tara Bella. They walked into a room where I saw my baby girl was napping. Anadhi was with her as she rocked the child.

Anadhi said, "Your mother couldn't name you, yet your Mama has named you Ahana Bella van Phillip and your big sister is Hana Bella van Phillip, daughters of Tara Bella and Andries van Phillip. Now remember, I am your Oma, and this is your forever home."

I saw Anadhi look at me directly and I knew she could see me. She said to me, "If you can see me and hear me, please know your children were adopted by my blessed son Andries and his wife Tara Bella. Andries is the brother of Jacobus and the brother and reincarnated son of Antonius."

Anadhi then said to me, "Tara Bella and Andries can't have any children of their own, so they were blessed as God has flown these two angels to them personally. Andries actually tells everyone a stock dropped the girls off to them as they flew and came to their parents."

I knew then Anadhi had taken care of everything for me as I had left a letter for her if I happened to pass away. I only wondered what had happened to Uncle James and Aunt Agatha, and Dr. David.

I then saw Uncle James and Aunt Agatha walk into the nursery. Uncle James took little Ahana Bella in his arms as Aunt Agatha held the hands of Hana Bella.

Uncle James kissed her and said, "I wish I could tell your Mom we are all right. My Anadhi wants us to stay with her for a while until you both get settled in or we get the courage to go back home. I would miss your mother so much, I don't know if I could go back there so quickly."

Kasteel Vrederic felt like it was full of people as then I saw my friend Rietje come and look at me. She walked to me as she called me and said, "Hi Ahana, I knew you were coming. But don't worry! Everyone is doing all right! I can have Papa tell you. Just wait here."

The whole family came and sat in the courtyard where I had passed away centuries ago. It felt so good though to be back here. I waited for someone to talk as I felt like words failed me or we were being pulled somewhere and had very little time.

Jacobus walked in and saw me. He said "Ahana, in this castle all types of miracles happen. You should know your children are now our children. The house is blessed now as our home is full of children. Dr. David is traveling around the globe trying to help all children, and victims of rape, molestation, and child sex trafficking, and give them free medical checkups. We have donated all the money Mr. Hunter had left to provide for and help stop child brides. You must travel and rise again with the knowledge your sacrifice was not in vain as we have started something."

I watched everyone as I saw then we were both back near the Sands Point Lighthouse. Frederic and I sat on the banks of the Long Island shore and knew this is where we both would like to be reborn from for this is where my story began as a child bride. I had only eighteen years to live on Earth, yet I wanted my years to be known as the years that had changed the lives of child brides around the world.

I lived and died for a cause I believe in, yet no one knew as it had been hidden in the basements of so many houses. I will rise like a phoenix from the ashes as my story continues to take rebirth on Earth over and over again, as child brides are being sent out every day as sex workers.

I know other courageous women too will fight this crisis as the night predators sit and wait with candy and toys in their hands to bait yet another child bride. I know as long as there are girls who fight them even slowly, we shall let all know we are resilient, and we will wipe this Earth of having any more child brides.

I watched the stars shining in the skies near the Sands Point Lighthouse as I heard the nightingales sing for us. We both went to the middle of the Long Island Sound as we joined together in an embrace and created the rising phoenix. Like a burning fire, we both became big and flew up to the skies from the ocean to rise once more as twin flames.

I heard a fisherman say, "I feel like I saw a pair of love birds were joined together over there rising from the ashes."

RISING FROM THE ASHES

In life, I found sorrow

And pain.

In life, I

Lived

With

Shattered

Wings.

I ached for kindness.

I yearned understanding.

I found nothing,

Yet

Tonight

In death,

I have found you

For you waited

Lovingly

For me.

You were happy

To wait till

Times

End

As you said,

Love is eternal.

Neither life

Nor death

Could separate

Twin flames

From one another,

For I promised

You,

I would wait

For only you,

Until

Times end.

Yet as

Our love found its course,

As our love was accepted

By the Heaven above,

The Earth beyond,

This is proof

We the true lovers,

In life

Or in death,

Will be united

Eternally.

Never cry,

Never worry

For true lovers,

True twin flames

Are never dead

As their love story

Is never finished.

We never say

The end

As we the twin flames

For one another,

With one another,

Are never dead as

Eternally we,

Are always

RISING FROM THE ASHES.

CONCLUSION:

Tara Bella's Children

"A mother is not defined by giving birth as a mother is defined by a mother's love and a child's call."

I am Tara Bella van Phillip. I have decided to fill in the conclusion chapter of Ahana's diary. The diary was miraculously filled up even after Ahana Roy left this Earth and went into the reincarnation zone. This diary, like a miracle, appeared in my house. It had a note which read:

"To be gifted to Tara Bella and her children. The Mama and Piano Papa my daughter Hana had known from the time she learned to talk even though I had no clue who they were."

So, this chapter I named Tara Bella's Children. I am the Mama my daughter was calling out for and my husband Andries actually is a world-renowned pianist, and we are lucky to be the parents of our beloved Ahana's children. I am blessed to have known a child bride who rose and fought the cruel world for her rights. She wanted to live in this world as a child. She wanted someone to provide her food and not go to bed hungry.

So, at a very young age, Ahana was married off. She was happy thinking this playhouse doll show would end soon and she would go home with Barbie dolls to play with. She did get her Barbie dolls, but not the kind a child would want.

The dolls she was given had to be carried within her womb for nine months. A child carried children, because she was married off to a monster. Her monster rapist was no prince in shining armor who came on a horse to take her away. Rather, he kept her as a prisoner in his basement.

For years, she saw no one. Neither did she know the big and busy New York City where she lived was full of people who never heard her screams nor saw her tears. Her childhood was robbed and the fear was instilled as she saw other child brides being sold off as sex workers. Never did she fear for herself as she took her destiny as her faith. A mother was awakened in the body of the small child bride. She found her voice after she turned eighteen years old. A mother became a protector and she fought the rich and famous, the privileged and the unjust leaders of this world who hide under the rugs of privilege.

A small voice became loud as it kept on buzzing until one by one, other humans heard her cries. No one wants to help the destitute, the rape victims, the abused, the battered, the victims of sex trafficking, and the child brides. The truth remains that these child brides enter rich countries from poverty-ridden areas as they are sold as brides. These girls are then sold as sex workers. Their lives remain within the pages of the unknown and the unheard.

The short-lived life story of Ahana Roy did appear on the newspapers. It was circulated on various social media websites, yet very quickly it became yesterday's news. No interest was gained from this news event. No one wanted to read or talk about social issues involving humanitarian crises. The solution in everyone's mind is let the other person deal with it.

Yet it's an issue where children are also stolen from their parents. The story of Ahana could also have been maybe, she was stolen from her family, not sold. Neither did she remember, nor will we ever know the complete truth. Let's not let another story be circulated in tomorrow's newspapers where we read about another child bride who was murdered.

Let's do something today and let's all keep our eyes out for the children of this world. Even if your neighbor shuts his doors to you, keep your doors open to make sure another child is not being hurt by anyone. Let the children live. Let them find a mother and a father who await their arrival.

I found my blessed daughters as they were fighting for their lives. My baby girls were born from a very brave and honorable mother's womb, a mother who fought to give them a different life than her own.

Today, my girls carry their birth mother's name and my name in their own names. I will be their mother eternally who found them as God's eternal blessings. Yet I will retell them the story of their brave mother who loved them everlastingly even beyond her death.

My babies are sleeping on top of my heart. Both my daughters had heart murmurs that their Big Papa Jacobus miraculously healed. Now I can every night hear both of their heartbeats and make sure they beat with love and joy. As my heart beats their names, I can feel their heartbeats and they keep me alive as I know my girls will be remembered as gifts from a child bride. They both have their two mothers' blessings upon them, and this world will never call them adopted babies as they are and shall be known as Tara Bella's Children.

TARA BELLA'S CHILDREN

Mother is defined not through

Birth,

Nor through

Blood,

As I shall

Carry you my beloved

Children

Not for

Nine months,

But as long

As it

Takes you to learn

To walk.

For even after that,

My babies, I shall

Carry you.

I shall protect you in my

Arms.

I will keep your heartbeats

Beating

Through

My

Love

And my prayers.

For my children, you

Are my gifts,

My prayers

Answered

As I asked,

I sought,

And I knocked

For you,

And that's how

You came to me.

For me,

You were given.

For me, you were sent

To this Earth.

Through the

Door

Of prayers

And the door of miracles,

I am blessed

As your mother gave

Birth to you

For me,

And from

This day forward

And eternally,

My children,

You shall be known

As

TARA BELLA'S CHILDREN.

DWELLERS WITHIN THE DIARY OF A CHILD BRIDE

Ahana Roy	Child bride, and birth mother of Hana Bella van Phillip and Ahana Bella van Phillip. Reincarnated form of seventeenth-century Ahana and twin flame of Frederic van der Bijl.
Frederic van der Bijl	Ghost sailor, seventeenth-century Dutch Naval Captain, cousin of seventeenth-century Sir Alexander van der Bijl, and twin flame of Ahana Roy.
Hana Bella van Phillip	Biological daughter of Ahana Roy and adopted daughter of Andries van Phillip and Tara Bella van Phillip.
Ahana Bella van Phillip	Biological daughter of Ahana Roy and adopted daughter of Andries van Phillip and Tara Bella van Phillip.
Agatha Newhouse Brown "Aunt Agatha"	Twin flame and wife of James Brown. Nurse and former nun, grandaunt of Anadhi Newhouse van Phillip, and descendant of the family of Aunt Marinda.

James Brown "Uncle James"	Twin flame and husband of Agatha Newhouse Brown. Dreamer, seeker, dream psychic, and preacher.
Mr. Hunter	Child sex trafficker.
Mrs. Hunter "The Lady"	Child sex trafficker.
Lisa	Child sex trafficker.
Senator	Child sex trafficker.
Dr. David van Peters	Friend of Dr. Jacobus Vrederic van Phillip.
Dr. Mandy van Peters	Child sex trafficker.
Dr. Johnathan Anderson	Emergency room physician.
Dr. Jacobus Vrederic van Phillip	Medical doctor with multiple specialties, and one-of-a-kind specialist in never-done-before transplant surgeries. Son of Erasmus van Phillip and Anadhi Newhouse van Phillip, cousin of Antonius van Phillip and Andries van Phillip, uncle of reincarnated Andries van Phillip and Griet Vrederic van Phillip, twin flame and husband of Dr. Margriete van Achthoven, and father of Rietje Vrederic van Phillip. Reincarnated form of sixteenth

and seventeenth-century Jacobus van Vrederic.

Dr. Margriete van Achthoven	Medical doctor, cardiologist, and pediatric cardiovascular surgeon. Co-owner of Agatha and Marinda's Orphanage. Twin flame and wife of Dr. Jacobus Vrederic van Phillip, and mother of Rietje Vrederic van Phillip. Reincarnated form of sixteenth and seventeenth-century Margriete van Wijck.
Anadhi Newhouse van Phillip	Author. Daughter of Dr. Andrew Newhouse and Dr. Gita Shankar Newhouse, granddaughter of Martin Newhouse and Miranda Newhouse, granddaughter of Hari Shankar and Parvati Shankar, twin flame and wife of Erasmus van Phillip, mother of Dr. Jacobus Vrederic van Phillip, aunt and adoptive mother of Antonius van Phillip and Andries van Phillip, grandmother of reincarnated Andries van Phillip, Griet Vrederic van Phillip, and Rietje Vrederic van Phillip. Reincarnated form of sixteenth-century Mahalt.
Erasmus van Phillip	World-renowned painter, and twenty-first-century owner of Kasteel Vrederic. Son of Greta van Phillip, descendant of the van

Vrederic family, twin flame and husband of Anadhi Newhouse van Phillip, father of Dr. Jacobus Vrederic van Phillip, uncle and adoptive father of Antonius van Phillip and Andries van Phillip, and grandfather of reincarnated Andries van Phillip, Griet Vrederic van Phillip, and Rietje Vrederic van Phillip. Reincarnated form of sixteenth-century Johannes van Vrederic.

Antonius van Phillip World-renowned painter. Son of Petrus van Phillip and Giada Berlusconi van Phillip, nephew and adopted son of Erasmus van Phillip and Anadhi Newhouse van Phillip, twin brother of Andries van Phillip, cousin and adoptive brother of Dr. Jacobus Vrederic van Phillip, twin flame and husband of Katelijne Snaaijer van Phillip, and father of reincarnated Andries van Phillip and Griet Vrederic van Phillip.

Katelijne Snaaijer van Phillip Stepdaughter of Ghileyn Snaaijer, twin flame and wife of Antonius van Phillip, and mother of reincarnated Andries van Phillip and Griet Vrederic van Phillip.

Andries van Phillip Deceased world-renowned pianist, son of Petrus van Phillip and Giada Berlusconi van Phillip,

nephew and adopted son of
Erasmus van Phillip and Anadhi
Newhouse van Phillip, twin
brother of Antonius van Phillip,
and cousin and adoptive brother
of Dr. Jacobus Vrederic van
Phillip. Now reincarnated son of
Antonius van Phillip and
Katelijne Snaaijer van Phillip,
grandson of Erasmus van Phillip
and Anadhi Newhouse van
Phillip, nephew of Dr. Jacobus
Vrederic van Phillip and Dr.
Margriete van Achthoven van
Phillip, brother of Griet Vrederic
van Phillip, cousin of Rietje
Vrederic van Phillip, twin flame
and husband of Tara Bella, and
adoptive father of Hana Bella van
Phillip and Ahana Bella van
Phillip.

Tara Bella van   Daughter of Sitara Bella and
Phillip   Marcello Esposito, twin flame
and wife of Andries van Phillip,
and adoptive mother of Hana
Bella van Phillip and Ahana Bella
van Phillip.

Griet Vrederic van   Daughter of Antonius van Phillip
Phillip   and Katelijne Snaaijer van
Phillip, granddaughter of Erasmus
van Phillip and Anadhi Newhouse
van Phillip, niece of Dr. Jacobus
Vrederic van Phillip and Dr.
Margriete Achthoven, sister of

216

Andries van Phillip, and cousin of Rietje Vrederic van Phillip. Reincarnated form of sixteenth-century Griet van Jacobus.

Rietje Vrederic van Phillip Daughter of Dr. Jacobus Vrederic van Phillip and Dr. Margriete van Achthoven, granddaughter of Erasmus van Phillip and Anadhi Newhouse van Phillip, and cousin of Andries van Phillip and Griet Vrederic van Phillip. Reincarnated form of sixteenth and seventeenth-century Margriete "Rietje" Jacobus Peters.

Aunt Marinda Time traveler, spiritual seer, nurse, and herbalist from the sixteenth century in the present day. Co-owner of Agatha and Marinda's Orphanage. Sister of Agatha and Tabitha, adoptive guardian of Theunis and Alexander, and twin flame and wife of Kees van Vrederic.

Kees van Vrederic Son of Marinus van Vrederic and Sakina, brother of Johannes van Vrederic, and twin flame and husband of Marinda.

Theunis Peters Adopted son of Aunt Marinda. Adoptive brother of Alexander. Reincarnated form of sixteenth-century Theunis Peters.

Alexander van der Bijl Adopted son of Aunt Marinda. Adoptive brother of Theunis. Reincarnated form of sixteenth and seventeenth-century Sir Alexander van der Bijl. Cousin of seventeenth-century Frederic van der Bijl.

GLOSSARY

Get acquainted with some terms and places that were used in this book.

Bangla/Bengali   Official language in Bangladesh and one of the major languages in India.

Bangladesh   Country located in South Asia.

Death   End of life on Earth, when the body and soul separate. More information on death can be found in the book *Eternal Truth: The Tunnel Of Light* by Ann Marie Ruby.

Dhaka   Capital city of Bangladesh.

Dreams   REM (rapid eye movement) cycle is when a sleeping body can travel through dreams. Proven scientifically dreams can occur and people do travel during their dreams. However, their bodies do not leave their places. Major religions have mainly come through dreams. More information on dreams can be found in the book *Eternal Truth: The Tunnel Of Light* by Ann Marie Ruby.

Dutch Term refers to both the language spoken and the people in the Netherlands.

Egypt Country in North Africa.

Gallows A place commonly known where witches were hung to their death.

Hindi A language spoken in India.

India Officially the Republic of India, country located in South Asia, and the second most populated country in the world.

Karma Reaction to a person's actions throughout his or her life. One of the core beliefs of Hinduism and Buddhism.

Kasteel Vrederic Castle Vrederic is the home of the Van Vrederic and Van Phillip family in the *Kasteel Vrederic* series, spanning from the sixteenth century through the present.

Meditation Meditation, also known as Dhyana, is the concentration of the mind, body, and soul. The concept first appeared in the Vedas in Hinduism and has since evolved worldwide.

Miracles Unexpected gift that cannot be explained by science or medicine. More information on miracles can be found in the book *Eternal Truth: The Tunnel Of Light* by Ann Marie Ruby.

Naarden City in the province of North Holland in the Netherlands.

New York City Most populated city in the United States within the state of New York. The city includes the borough of Manhattan.

Niger Country in Africa.

Oma Grandmother in Dutch.

Opa Grandfather in Dutch.

Pakistan Country in South Asia.

Poffertjes Dutch pancakes.

Rabindranath Tagore Bengali Nobel Laureate.

Reincarnation/Rebirth Belief of a lot of people worldwide such as Buddhism, Hinduism, Jainism, Sikhism, and more. Today science can't disprove reincarnation. Also a lot of people have given proof of their rebirth. More information on reincarnation

can be found in the book
*Eternal Truth: The Tunnel Of
Light* by Ann Marie Ruby.

Sands Point   Village on Long Island within
the state of New York.

Spaniards   Members of the Spanish army
who fought for the King of
Spain.

Stakes   A place where witches were
burned to death.

Tunnel Of Light   Scientifically it is known as
the NDE (near-death
experience) tunnel. More
information on the tunnel of
light can be found in the book
*Eternal Truth: The Tunnel Of
Light* by Ann Marie Ruby.

Twin Flames   Research has shown twin
flames can survive as
individuals yet are complete in
union. More information on
twin flames can be found in
the book *Eternal Truth: The
Tunnel Of Light* by Ann Marie
Ruby.

Witch Hunts   A tribunal, heretical, and
shameful time for the world,
as innocent women or men
were accused of being witches
or warlocks, because someone
might have just accused the

person or the person could
have had some special gift.

ANN MARIE RUBY

MESSAGE FROM
THE AUTHOR

"Children are born as stars on Earth, they are the miraculous doors of hope, yet why is it some children cry upon a star floating in the sky wishing they too were a star in the eyes of their parents."

Children are the future of this world. They are our glimmering hope. Yet why is it even in this day and age we still have gender disparity? So many places around the globe still have unfair judgement regarding girls' rights. We all talk about so many human rights violations, yet I wonder does the world ever think about the child brides. What about their rights? Where in this world would they get justice?

Has this crisis landed in the International Court Of Justice yet? If not, maybe my fictional story of a child bride will awaken some cold-hearted souls. Maybe this book will churn inside the humans' inner souls and awaken all humans with humanity. As child marriages fall into the acts of human rights violations, it's a tragedy that has no ending. All girls subjected to being a child bride and those of whom are sold as sex workers were born with shattered wings.

They can't stand up for themselves for they have no voice. They have no future or present as they live each night to survive their ill fate for another day. Child marriages have caused these girls to become pregnant and have severe health issues. In this fictional story, Ahana Roy's mother had told her if only she was a boy, her fate would have been different.

In this time and age, there are over 650 million women who were child brides. To this day, one in every five girls are child brides. Just think of the statistics about this number. How many girls do you think are married off as a child bride each minute? The answer is twenty-eight girls.

I wonder have we moved on forward as a society or is it the women are still left behind? If so many of the girls are left behind because their wings are shattered, how is this society moving forward equally? Are these girls not a part of our society or is it that they don't even count as they all were born with shattered wings?

Tonight, if you are a parent or a sibling, or an aunt or uncle who has a newborn girl, hold on to her tightly. Somewhere on this Earth, a newborn baby is being sold off as a child bride. Hold that thought to yourself for a while.

Now go and think of that child and know she is Ahana. They all are called Ahanas of this world who have no future as they don't even count as members of this society. They live hidden somewhere in someone's basement. They give birth to more child brides who then face a cruel death. No head stones are laid for them. No memorials are held for them as their paths were covered with shattered glass.

They lived on Earth while their feet were bleeding yet they never told you anything. They were all taught at childhood, girls don't feel pain, they don't get hungry, nor should girls cry. Yet teardrops keep on falling. You the abusers can take all away from these girls, yet I ask you, why don't you then take their tears away from them? Take away their pain and their hunger, so then you won't have to ask them to not cry.

Today, there are a lot of laws that prevent child brides from being married off at a young age, yet it's still happening. The laws have loopholes and that's how the predators enter and the girls are still becoming child brides. Let's in union stop this unjust from happening to the girls of this world.

The good news is as we are more aware of this situation, child marriage is also in a slow decline. Ten years ago, one in every four girls were child brides. Now, one in every five girls are child brides. I want all of you to take this fictional story into the inner cores of your hearts and do something about this situation.

It hurts my inner core as I see there are children raising children. There are children who are being trafficked for sex. Please let all children be just that, children. Let them dream as teenagers and may they find their Frederics when the time is right.

I hope Ahana Roy has left her diary with all of us as a lesson taught. May her journey through this crisis not go in vain. I hope her children find a different life and grow up as admirable members of this society who will tell the world their mother was a child bride. She struggled through this catastrophic storm so they won't have to.

I have named this admirable woman Ahana because it means immortal and morning glory. In my eyes, she is immortal through the story of her life. She is like the morning glories that bloom in our gardens. They bloom in the morning and fall asleep at night for they have a short life, just like Ahana. Yet they awaken to bloom again to brighten up another day in another time, just like Ahana will be reborn again another day in another time.

I want everyone who is reading this book to share this story with a friend. Let's spread this story throughout all the streets of this one harmonious world. Let us in union end and eradicate child marriages from this world. For my brave and beloved Ahana, I want all of you to finish what she had started and help end this humanitarian crisis.

ABOUT THE AUTHOR

"Meet Ann Marie Ruby from San Francisco, California.
This is her story."

Ann Marie Ruby was born into a diplomatic family for which she had the privilege of traveling the world. This upbringing made the whole world her one family. She never saw a country as a foreign country yet as a neighbor who was there for her as she would be there for them. After all, isn't that what families do for one another?

Ann Marie became an author as she started to place her chosen words into the pages of her diaries. She knew she must collect all her thoughts and produce them into different diaries. Each diary became her different books.

Ann Marie's life goal is not to just write something but only what she believes in. So all her thoughts and words remained within the pages of her diaries until she realized it was time she must share them with you. Otherwise, she felt selfish and knew that was not her characteristic as she lives for everyone, not just for herself.

INTERNATIONAL #1 BESTSELLING AUTHOR:

Ann Marie became an international number-one bestselling author of twenty-three books. Alongside being a full-time author, she loves to write articles on her website where she can have a better connection with all of you. Ann Marie, a dream psychic, became a blogger and a humanitarian only because she believes in you and herself as a complete, honest, and open family.

PERSONAL:

Ann Marie is an American who grew up in Brisbane, Australia. She resided in the Washington, D.C. area, later settled in Seattle, Washington, and currently lives in San Francisco, California. In her spare time when she is not writing books, she loves to meditate, pray, listen to music, cook, and write blog posts.

BESTSELLING:

Ann Marie's books have placed her on top 100 bestselling charts in various countries including the Netherlands, United States, United Kingdom, Canada, and Germany. In 2020, she became a household name as her books began to consistently rank #1 on multiple bestselling charts. *The Netherlands: Land Of My Dreams* and *Everblooming: Through The Twelve Provinces Of The Netherlands*, both became overnight number-one bestsellers in the United States.

In 2020, *The Netherlands: Land Of My Dreams* also became a bestseller in the Netherlands and Canada, consistently becoming #1 on various lists and one of the top selling books on Amazon NL. *Everblooming: Through The Twelve Provinces Of The Netherlands* became #37 on the Netherlands top 100 bestselling Amazon books chart which includes all books from all genres. Ann Marie's other books have also made various top 100 bestselling lists and received multiple accolades including *Eternal Truth: The Tunnel Of Light* which was named as one of eight thought-provoking books by women.

ROMANCE FICTION:

Ann Marie's *Kasteel Vrederic* series was written in a diary fashion. She has always kept a diary herself, so she thought her characters too could keep a diary. All of their diaries became individual books yet collectively, they are a part of a family, the Kasteel Vrederic family.

OTHER BOOKS:

All of Ann Marie's nonfiction and fiction books are available globally. You can take a look at short descriptions about the books at the end of this book.

THE NETHERLANDS:

Ann Marie revealed why many of her books revolve around the Netherlands, sharing that as a dream psychic, she had seen the historical past of a country in her dreams and was later able to place a name to the country. This is described in detail in *Spiritual Lighthouse: The Dream Diaries Of Ann Marie Ruby* and *The Netherlands: Land Of My Dreams* where she also wrote about her plans to eventually move to the Netherlands.

Ann Marie has received letters on behalf of His Majesty King Willem-Alexander and Her Majesty Queen Máxima of the Netherlands after they received her books *The Netherlands: Land Of My Dreams* and *Everblooming: Through The Twelve Provinces Of The Netherlands*. Additionally, Ann Marie has received letters on behalf of His Excellency Mark Rutte, the Prime Minister of the Netherlands for her books.

WRITING:

Ann Marie also is acclaimed globally as one of the top voices in the spiritual space, however, she is recognized for her writing abilities published across many genres namely spirituality, lifestyle, inspirational quotations, poetry, fiction, romance, history, travel, social awareness, and more. Her writing style is hailed by critics and readers alike as making readers feel as though they have made a friend.

FOLLOW THE AUTHOR:

Now as you have found her book, why don't you and Ann Marie become friends? Join her and become a part of her global family. Ann Marie shall always give you books which you will read and then find yourself as a part of her book family.

For more information about Ann Marie Ruby, any one of her books, or to read her blog posts and articles, subscribe to her website, www.annmarieruby.com.

Follow Ann Marie Ruby on Twitter, Facebook, Instagram, Threads, and Pinterest:

@TheAnnMarieRuby

BOOKS BY THE AUTHOR

INSPIRATIONAL QUOTATIONS SERIES:

This series includes four books of original quotations and one omnibus edition.

Spiritual Travelers:
Life's Journey From The Past
To The Present
For The Future

Spiritual
Messages:
From A Bottle

Spiritual Journey:
Life's Eternal Blessings

Spiritual
Inspirations:
Sacred Words
Of Wisdom

Omnibus edition contains all four books of original quotations.

Spiritual Ark:
The Enchanted Journey Of Timeless
Quotations

SPIRITUAL SONGS SERIES:

This series includes two original spiritual prayer books.

SPIRITUAL SONGS: LETTERS FROM MY CHEST

When there was no hope, I found hope within these sacred words of prayers, I but call songs. Within this book, I have for you, 100 very sacred prayers.

SPIRITUAL SONGS II: BLESSINGS FROM A SACRED SOUL

Prayers are but the sacred doors to an individual's enlightenment. This book has 123 prayers for all humans with humanity.

SPIRITUAL LIGHTHOUSE: THE DREAM DIARIES OF ANN MARIE RUBY

Do you believe in dreams? For within each individual dream, there is a hidden message and a miracle interlinked. Learn the spiritual, scientific, religious, and philosophical aspects of dreams. Walk with me as you travel through forty nights, through the pages of my book.

THE WORLD HATE CRISIS: THROUGH THE EYES OF A DREAM PSYCHIC

Humans have walked into an age where humanity now is being questioned as hate crimes have reached a catastrophic amount. Let us in union stop this crisis. Pick up my book and see if you too could join me in this fight.

ETERNAL TRUTH: THE TUNNEL OF LIGHT

Within this book, travel with me through the doors of birth, death, reincarnation, true soulmates and twin flames, dreams, miracles, and the end of time.

THE NETHERLANDS: LAND OF MY DREAMS

Oh the sacred travelers, be like the mystical river and journey through this blessed land through my book. Be the flying bird of wisdom and learn about a land I call, Heaven on Earth.

EVERBLOOMING: THROUGH THE TWELVE PROVINCES OF THE NETHERLANDS

Original poetry and hand-picked tales are bound together in this keepsake book. Come travel with me as I take you through the lives of the Dutch past.

LOVE LETTERS:
THE TIMELESS
TREASURE

Fifty original timeless treasured love poems are presented with individual illustrations describing each poem.

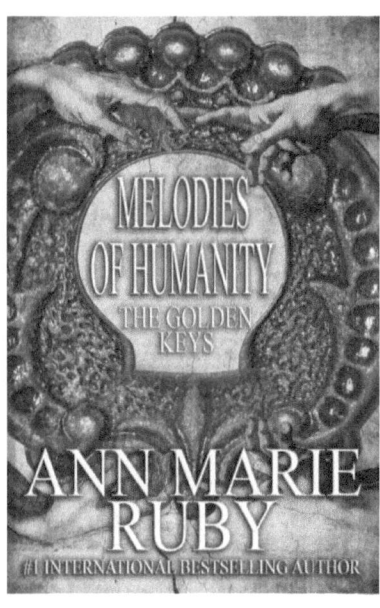

MELODIES OF
HUMANITY:
THE GOLDEN KEYS

Thirty-two poems retell the melodies of humanity, calling all humans to awaken their humanity through love, the golden keys everyone carries within their inner souls.

KASTEEL VREDERIC SERIES:

ETERNALLY BELOVED: I SHALL NEVER LET YOU GO

Travel time to the sixteenth century where Jacobus van Vrederic, a beloved lover and father, surmounts time and tide to find the vanished love of his life. On his pursuit, Jacobus discovers secrets that will alter his life evermore. He travels through the Eighty Years' War-ravaged country, the Netherlands as he takes the vow, even if separated by a breath, "Eternally beloved, I shall never let you go."

EVERMORE BELOVED: I SHALL NEVER LET YOU GO

Jacobus van Vrederic returns with the devoted spirits of Kasteel Vrederic. A knight and a seer also join him on a quest to find his lost evermore beloved. They journey through a war-ravaged country, the Netherlands, to stop another war which was brewing silently in his land, called the witch hunts. Time was his enemy as he must defeat time and tide to find his evermore beloved wife alive.

BE MY DESTINY: VOWS FROM THE BEYOND

Fighting their biggest enemy destiny, twin flames Erasmus van Phillip and Anadhi Newhouse are reborn over and over again only to lose the battle to destiny. Find out if through the helping hands of sacred spirits of the sixteenth century, these eternal twin flames are finally able to unite in the twenty-first century, as they say, "Reincarnation is a blessing if only you are mine."

HEART BEATS YOUR NAME: VOWS FROM THE BEYOND

While one is sleepless, the other twin flame is sleeping eternally. Now how does Antonius van Phillip awaken his twin flame Katelijne Snaaijer from beyond Earth, and solve a murder mystery, she is the only witness to yet also a victim of? Find out how the musical sound of heartbeats guide him to his sleeping beloved while he solves the mystery sleepless.

ENTRANCED BELOVED: I SHALL NEVER LET YOU GO

The pages of Margriete "Rietje" Jacobus Peters's love story from her diary slowly go missing from the library of Kasteel Vrederic. The twenty-first-century descendants fighting death and time must travel back in time to save their ancestors and their beloved Kasteel Vrederic. Traveling through the tunnel of light, the family of the twenty-first century must save the seventeenth-century twin flames. Rietje and her beloved twin flame Sir Alexander van der Bijl must create another paranormal, magical, historical, romantic diary for the dynasty to even exist.

FORBIDDEN DAUGHTER OF KASTEEL VREDERIC: VOWS FROM THE BEYOND

Jacobus Vrederic van Phillip stopped pouring tears and burning himself with memories of passion to become a stone, so he could live with memories and not recreate new ones. The Vrederic family members realize the curse of past life's karma will come and meet them in this life and erase the only child who kept the dynasty going, the child known to all as the forbidden daughter of Kasteel Vrederic. The man who has sacrificed his life for all members of his family and society now must find a way to awaken his sleeping soul, recognize his twin flame, and bring back as the beloved daughter the only child he had rejected. To this world she was known as the forbidden daughter of Kasteel Vrederic.

THE IMMORTALITY SERUM: VOWS FROM THE BEYOND

Andries van Phillip, the famous pianist, gets calls from his dead twin flame Tara Bella in his dreams. All dressed in red, she roams around a burning castle trying to rescue all the people from within, without realizing she was the victim, not Andries. Now the paranormal family travels across the ocean as they fight Succubus the demoness, rescue the woman in red, and solve a murder mystery, all while they know before time ends, they must find the immortality serum.

WOMAN IN THE MIRROR: VOWS FROM THE BEYOND

The eighth book in this series is coming soon.

Coming Soon

WOMAN IN THE MIRROR: VOWS FROM THE BEYOND

BRIDE OF THE IMMORTAL: VOWS FROM THE BEYOND

The ninth book in this series is coming soon.

Coming Soon

BRIDE OF THE IMMORTAL: VOWS FROM THE BEYOND

SHATTERED WINGS: DIARY OF A CHILD BRIDE

Ahana Roy fought this unkind world to make room for her in this society, where she would not go to bed hungry. She was brought to the city of dreams where her dreams were shattered as she became a child bride. How will she fight the war of being a child bride in a city that has no idea of her existence? In her shattered dreams, she found a ghost sailor who promised to be with her, dead or alive. Following the advice of a dead sailor, Ahana wandered the streets of New York City looking for help. There she found the paranormal family of Kasteel Vrederic as her helping hands. This is the diary of child bride who said, "I had no chance in life as I was born with shattered wings."

ENCHANTED TALES: A KASTEEL VREDERIC STORYBOOK FOR CHILDREN

Travel around the world in seven nights. Through enchanted tales you will meet and assist superheroes from the seven continents of this world. While there, you will learn about different cultures and landmarks. Keep your magical lanterns glowing as you help the girl with the lantern solve mysteries around the globe.

Coming Soon

BROTHER BEAR AND THE FOUR INVESTIGATORS: A KASTEEL VREDERIC STORYBOOK FOR CHILDREN

BROTHER BEAR AND THE FOUR INVESTIGATORS: A KASTEEL VREDERIC STORYBOOK FOR CHILDREN

Kasteel Vrederic's second storybook is coming soon.

www.ingramcontent.com/pod-product-compliance
Lightning Source LLC
Chambersburg PA
CBHW050729180626
46814CB00002B/670